A.K.A. KIDNEY MAN

A.K.A. KIDNEY MAN

JUDY VOIGT
AND
KAREN LoBELLO

COVER ART BY KAT TATZ

Printed in the United States of America

ISBN: 978-1-7351603-0-6 (paperback)
ISBN: 978-1-7351603-1-3 (ebook)

Book design by TeaBerryCreative.com

Inspired by Nick,
the original Kidney Man

ACKNOWLEDGEMENTS

COOKIE CIRKOSZ

We give a special nod of thanks to Nick's Mom, Cookie Cirkosz, for sharing personal stories about Nick. We value her input and insight in answering our many questions.

DR. BRUCE MORGENSTERN

Our goal was to highlight the importance of organ donation and accurately portray chronic kidney disease, which affects thousands of people of all ages every day. Pediatric nephrologist, Dr. Bruce Morgenstern, guided us throughout this process. We are forever grateful to him for sharing his wealth of knowledge. Before he moved to Las Vegas to help start the Roseman College of Medicine, he was the medical director of the kidney transplant program at Phoenix Children's Hospital.

ANN CREEL
Our sincere thanks to our editor, Ann Creel, for her thorough and thoughtful critique of A.K.A. *Kidney Man*. It was a plus that she had once worked as an RN in a dialysis unit. She went the extra mile, and we appreciated it.

KAT TATZ
The cover of our book is a work of art by our dear friend, Kat Tatz. Her talent is amazing...and we're glad she's so patient! KatTatz.com

THE NATIONAL KIDNEY FOUNDATION
Thank you to *The National Kidney Foundation* for the invaluable information. A portion of the book profits will be donated to this foundation: *www.kidney.org*.

FOURTH GRADERS AT CHARLOTTE HILL ELEMENTARY SCHOOL
Many thanks to Judy's fourth grade students who were the first kids to hear A.K.A. *Kidney Man* when it was still a manuscript. Their excitement for our story and characters meant everything to us.

FAMILY AND FRIENDS
Last—but far from least—many thanks to our husbands, Rich and Barry, Judy's sons, Nick and Matt, and our siblings, nieces and nephews, relatives, colleagues

and friends who made up our core group of first readers. We thank you all for your enthusiasm and valuable
feedback. Your support means more than you know!

Carol Dweck: "*Growth Mindset*" *(2015)*
Quotes derived from Dr. Seuss: www.seussville.com

CHAPTER ONE

> "I'm sorry to say so,
> but sadly it's true
> that bang-ups and hang-ups
> can happen to you."
> —DR. SEUSS

I am Nicholas Robert Cicero, but you can call me *Kidney Man*. Who knew those two little words would change my life forever.

Mom's hand touched my forehead...probably checking for a fever. "Nicholas...time to get up." I'd been sick for a week, and—for the record—having the flu is no joke.

I not only felt horrible for seven straight days, but I also couldn't have Diego over for our usual Friday night sleepover ritual: a marathon bike ride to the park, an equally long video-game session, pizza delivery, and my favorite drink...ice-cold Pepsi. *I guess there's always next week.*

I still didn't feel a hundred percent, but I knew I had to go back to school at some point. I opened one eye long enough to see my dog, Velcro, staring back at me. I rolled out of bed and onto the floor as he jumped on me, licking away. You would've thought I had cheese on my cheeks.

As we moved into the bathroom, he watched me like a hawk. "Are you taking notes, Velcro?" I think he wanted me to clear out so *he* could get ready too. I gave my face and teeth a once over, cleaned my glasses, made sure my cowlick wasn't sticking straight up like a Mohawk, and headed downstairs. *Mission accomplished.*

Next stop, the kitchen. Mom whistled for Velcro to give him his morning treat. As for me, the waffles called my name. But when I opened the freezer, I realized they must've called Eddie's name a little louder. "Mom...he did it again!" Nothing but an empty box. I could picture my big brother's satisfied face. Good thing he doesn't like cereal...at least he didn't wipe that out.

Mom tossed the hollow container in the trash and tried to make me less annoyed. "I'll pick up more at the store today."

I poured a giant helping of Cheerios and was about to add a big scoop of sugar when I eyed her watching me. She cleared her throat, no doubt a reminder of last week's threat about going overboard with the white stuff. "I know…I know…I'll put some back…"

I wolfed down a banana, then fired up my favorite video and waited. Just as the last slurp of milk vanished from the bottom of the bowl, my best friend, Diego, rang the doorbell. He doesn't have far to walk 'cause he lives right next door. The first day we moved into the neighborhood, he knocked at the door and asked my dad, "Any kids live here?" We've been best friends ever since. I gave him a nickname right away…now he's A.K.A. (that's also known as) D. It just rolls off the tongue.

I opened the squeaky old screen door and asked my usual, "*¿Qué pasa, amigo?*" I wanted to get comfortable using the Spanish words his grandma had taught me.

"*Nada. Estoy bien.*" I looked at D with my confused-about-Spanish-words look. He wrinkled his forehead. "That means I'm fine, dude. Now let's move it. We can't be late again." He smiled and came in for a high-five. "My *abuela* will be proud of you though." *That's a fact.*

The coast was clear, so we took a detour to the cookie jar, shoved handfuls of vanilla wafers into our mouths and yelled a quick goodbye to Mom as the door slammed behind us.

In the distance we heard, "Have a good day, boys…"

We made it to school with no time to spare. The principal, Mr. Vanasco, wrapped up the announcements over the loudspeaker just as Sam, also known as Bam, busted into class, his hair sticking out in a hundred different directions. *And I thought my cowlick was bad.* He handed our teacher a blue late slip as he mumbled a "Sorry, Miss T." Combs aren't his thing, but football sure is. In fact, every time he throws a pass...*Bam!*...he hits his target—which is why I gave him that nickname.

Miss Taylor signaled Jamal to tap a drum roll on his desk. *Hmm...what does she have up her sleeve?* "Class, remember when we read the story of *Romeo and Juliet* a couple weeks ago?" We all mumbled in agreement. "Well, today I have actual scripts for you to look at." As she passed out copies, we all buzzed with excitement about holding a real script to a play.

Miss Taylor said, "At the end of the year, our class will perform this on the big stage in the multipurpose room. The art teacher already said he'd make us a fake balcony."

Bam blurted out, "The balcony scene is a big deal, isn't it?"

"That's right, Sam. In William Shakespeare's famous play, it's the one audiences look forward to the most." She quickly followed up with, "We'll read it through today, then put it aside for a while. I won't assign parts for a couple weeks." She chuckled at our gargantuan, group groan.

When we reached the second act, I started to wish I *had* stayed home one more day. My skin was clammy, and my body felt weak and jittery. I thought about laying my head on the desk, but I didn't want to get in trouble. I took my glasses off and laid *them* on the desk instead. They must've weighed fifty pounds.

My hands shook. My hair dripped with sweat. I wanted to jump up and bolt to the restroom, but balancing on two pieces of boiled spaghetti wouldn't work. The room started spinning, and I needed a drink of water—fast.

Then it happened…The last thing I heard was that famous line, "Romeo, Romeo…wherefore art thou?…" before everything went black.

CHAPTER TWO

**"Step with care and great tact
And remember that life's a great balancing act."**
—DR. SEUSS

I heard a lot of commotion. The sound was muffled, and I wasn't even sure where I was. "NICHOLAS...CAN YOU HEAR ME?"

I tried so hard to wake up, but my eyelids wouldn't cooperate. In fact, they stuck together like two sheets of paper dipped in super glue. When they finally cracked open, I was looking straight up at the nose hairs of my fifth-grade teacher...not a pretty sight. And, as nice as she is, Miss Taylor might want to rethink that blue glittery stuff on her eyelids. The pain in my head helped me remember the whole ugly scene, and I have to say...it felt like I just tumbled off Juliet's balcony.

I heard Diego's voice. "What the heck happened? Nick's on the ground."

My teacher snapped. "Grab my radio...he fainted." *They're talking about me? I fainted?*

"Maybe I should just call 9-1-1?" Diego always wished he could dial 9-1-1.

"I think the nurse will know just what to do."

I lay there, staring silently...searching her eyes for an explanation of what had just happened. All she said was, "Hang in there, Nick."

I couldn't muster up much volume, but I made a pitiful attempt to speak. "Am I bleeding?" She apparently didn't hear me. *Feels like I'm dying here...right in the middle of room 19...Sheesh.* Tears rolled down my cheeks.

A bunch of kids hovered over me like I was part of a crime scene. Fortunately, we weren't allowed to use phones in class; otherwise, the most horrible moment of my life would've been plastered all over social media.

As if things couldn't get worse, I heard Molly Cooper ask, "Is he still breathing?" Even when she doesn't make sense, she still runs her big mouth. She didn't get to be president of the B.S. for nothing. That's the Bigmouth Society. I know...kind of harsh...but if the shoe fits...and, for the record, she's no Cinderella.

My buddy, Eli, who's way smarter than the rest of us put together, set her straight. "Don't you think Miss Taylor would do CPR if Nick quit breathing?" *Duh. Score one for the professor.* I dubbed him that 'cause he never runs out of facts. He whispered in his most irritated voice, "...and zip it, Molly...he can probably hear you."

Before she could answer, the teacher said, "Everyone head back to your seats. Nick needs some space." *Yes...please...back off.*

"Ewww...! He got blood on my desk!" Molly's voice pierced my ears. "I'm not going to clean that up 'cause I didn't do it...and it got all over my brand new pencil!"

I couldn't believe I was laid out flat on the floor, and all she cared about was her precious pink pencil. *Excuse me...I'm the one with the problem here!*

Bam said, "Geez, Molly. He didn't do it on purpose."

"Okay, guys. Let's all settle down." Miss Taylor was a bit frazzled.

Nurse Abby came into the room and took right over. I felt relieved. "Hold this piece of gauze on your cut, Nicholas. Keep pressure on it while I put some tape on there."

"Okay..." My voice sounded a bit stronger. "I already got blood on Molly's desk." *We don't need a repeat of that scene.*

"Oh dear..." She glanced at my teacher.

"Don't worry about that," Miss T said caringly. "I'll ask the custodian to clean it up."

The nurse put me in the wheelchair she kept in her office. I always thought it would be cool to ride in that thing, but I was way wrong on that one. If you're in it, you're sick or hurt.

As we got to the end of the hall, I could tell my friend, George, was in the health office. I *heard* him long before I *saw* him. He sneezed four times in a row, and he almost always goes to eight. Don't even think about saying *gesundheit* until he's done. That's why I nicknamed him Sneezy—like the dwarf. The professor thinks that moniker, as he calls it, is perfect for George because sneezing that many times in a row without stopping makes him worthy of it.

Sneezy looked shocked to see me in the new ride. "What happened to you?"

Nurse Abby answered for me. "Our boy here passed out in the classroom."

"Oh, wow! Are you okay?" George is the kind of guy you can cry in front of; he won't tell anybody.

"A little rattled...I smacked my head on Molly's desk." I reached up and touched the bloody bandage, just in case he didn't notice it.

"Nice aim!" He knows how I feel about Molly.

Even though my entire body was wobbly, I managed a grin.

"Well, I hope you feel better..." Sneezy headed back to class. Nurse Abby helped me onto the leather-padded treatment table against the back wall of the health office. That's where she fixed everybody up.

She took a closer look at the cut on my head, wiped it with something that stung a little and said, "I'll move some of that dirty blond hair out of the way so this bandage doesn't stick to it."

"My hair's not dirty. I just washed it last night." *I think I did.*

She chuckled, "Oh no, Nick. I was talking about the *color* dirty blond." *We can chalk that stupid comment up to my head injury.* "Did you eat breakfast this morning?"

"A little. Some Cheerios and part of a banana." I conveniently forgot to mention the handful of wafers and the extra sugar on my cereal. "I wanted an apple-cinnamon waffle, but my brother ate the last one." My big brother doesn't even like waffles, but he does like to annoy me every chance he gets.

Nurse Abby got a phone call, then turned to me and said, "I'll be back in about ten minutes." She examined my eyes one more time. "Miss Sandi's here, if you need anything. I have to check on another student." As she walked to the door, she said, "By the way, that was your mom on the phone. She'll be here soon."

I stretched out on the cushioned table and stared at the ceiling. Every few minutes I checked to see if my bandage was still on. *Did my hands quit shaking? Not yet.*

I thought about how crazy this morning was and decided it definitely could've been worse, 'cause thankfully...yeah, I'm still breathing, Molly.

CHAPTER THREE

*"You're in pretty good shape
for the shape you are in."*
—DR. SEUSS

When Mom finally picked me up from school, I begged her to let me go home and just keep a bandaid on my cut. But she dragged me to the pediatrician's office, just like I thought she would. "We're in luck, Nick...Dr. Katz can fit you in right now."

That's what she calls luck? "Will I get jabbed with a needle?" I don't like shots and shots don't like me.

"Nicholas, this visit isn't for shots. It's to see why you passed out in the middle of class. We also want to be sure you didn't get a concussion when you hit your head."

It did still hurt quite a bit.

The nurse called us back quickly, but before we went to an exam room, we made a pit stop. I had to go into the bathroom and pee in a plastic cup. Weird. *Wait till D hears this one.* Down the hall was the zoo animal exam room. Why do I always feel like a two-year-old there? Must be the murals. I mean, as far as I know, giraffes and alligators don't even smile, so why paint them that way? I don't mind the solar system exam room...at least those walls are decorated with planets and constellations.

Before I could even get comfortable in *Kiddie City*, they shuffled us off to a tiny little cubicle...one I'd never been in. *Make up your mind, people.* The lady in there told me her name was Viola. She said, "I'm what you call a phlebotomist."

I mean, I know my brain's a little foggy today, but...fla-bot-o-what?

"I'm going to take blood from you and send it to the lab so a scientist can examine it under a microscope."

"Cool...I love science."

She quickly printed off a bunch of stickers labeled with my name.

"Go ahead and raise your sleeve up for me, so I can find a good vein." She pointed to a spot on my arm. "See that light blue line? That's a good one."

"It is?"

She wrapped an elastic band around the top of my arm. "I think so..." Then she wiped the area to get rid of germs. "There...your vein is popping right out for me."

"Is this gonna hurt?"

"Nope, but it might pinch for a second. You can look away if you want." *Thank you very much…needles freak me out.*

The poke of the needle made me shrink back a little, expecting pain. It wasn't as bad as I thought it might be though. I was more interested in what she was doing than how I felt. She filled those little tubes like a contestant in a blood-sucking contest. *Viola the Vampire.*

She stepped out of the room for a second, so I grabbed my phone and took a one-handed photo of the vials. I wanted proof in case the kids didn't believe how much blood she took.

I sat there for a while to make sure I wasn't going to pass out again, then we headed back to the zoo. Dr. Katz came in and looked over my chart. He pressed all over my stomach. There was a spot or two where I let out a little "Ouch." He shined his flashlight in my eyes and said he was looking at my brain. *Really?* Then he spoke to Mom. "We'll know more when we get Nick's test results back." I tried to read his face, but he didn't give any clues.

My mother wouldn't let him escape just yet. "Does his head look okay?"

"It's a small abrasion…nothing serious." He got up to leave. "I'll put a rush on the test results, Mrs. Cicero, and give you a call when I get them back…probably tomorrow morning." Since he ruled out a concussion, I figured the results must have something to do with my pit stop or my missing blood. Vampire lady…*grrr…*

⚡

We finally made it home. Gram sat watching her game shows on TV. I headed straight for her 'cause I knew there'd be a hug waiting. She's good at hugs. No favor was ever too big to ask of Grandma. She'd do anything to help. No matter what. "Hi, sweet pea." I wouldn't let anyone but Gram get away with calling me *that*. "Come and lie on the couch with me and look at this crazy puzzle. Maybe we can solve it together." She loves to figure out which letters fill the boxes after they spin that wheel. I was worn out, so I gladly did what she said. "How are you feeling, honey?"

I gave her a look that meant *Not too great*. She covered me with my favorite blanket. Not like a "blankie" or anything, but it was a soft one that felt good.

I saw right away that I got out of having a tea party with my little sister, Katie. Since Dad was at the Atlanta airport waiting for his return flight from a business trip, Grandma and Grandpa stayed with Katie while Mom took me to the doctor's office. Pops—that's what I call my grandfather—can't say no to "his little princess," that's for sure. Last week, he let her put a crown from *Burger King* on his head. He even wore it into the grocery store. She tried to stick that same crown on Velcro's head, but he made a run for his doggie door. He's no dummy, but he is nosy. That's how he got his name…he sticks his nose in everything.

Pops came over to the couch after he escaped tea party duty. "Hey, buddy. You've had one heck of a day!"

"Yeah," I said...but I could barely hear my own voice, and I wasn't even trying to be dramatic.

His eyes shifted from me to my mom as she walked into the family room. "He'll be fine, Maureen. He's looking better already." I could tell Grandpa just said that so Mom wouldn't worry. He always tells her she's a natural born worrier. From the look on her face, he might be right. "You know, Maur...Shakespeare wrote a line in a play that says, 'Worry is an old man's game.'"

I said, "Hey, that's from the play we're reading in class." Nobody even heard me.

Mom kidded, "Speaking of old men, you should talk, Dad...I learned from the best."

Pops chuckled. "*Touché*..."

"I'll feel better once the doctor calls with those test results." She went into the kitchen and yelled out something about sticking around for dinner.

"What do you think, Bonnie?" Pops asked Grandma if she wanted to stay, but we all knew the answer. No one turns down Mom's cooking. She makes the best lasagna.

Katie headed toward me, dragging a slew of dolls along with her, and that usually meant one thing.

In her four-year-old voice she said, "Nick, pwetty please, will you play with me?" I always feel bad when I have to say no to my sister. She's a master at guilt trips.

Gram stroked Katie's hair behind her ears. My sister looked like a hot mess. Grandma fixed her ribbon and said, "Honey, your brother needs to rest...he just saw Dr. Katz." *Gram to the rescue.*

Katie felt my forehead like Mom does when we're sick. "Do you need a juice box, Nick?" She thinks a juice box will fix anything.

Gram answered for me again. "He'll be okay. He's just tired."

"My dolly has to go to the doctaw today too. I'll be wight back." As she took off, she made a pretend siren sound and just about knocked Pops over as her ambulance turned the corner, so he plopped down next to me.

He tapped one of his fists on top of mine which signaled our special handshake:

Two fist bumps.
Slap hands up high.
Then slap down low.
Salute.

I couldn't give it my all, but we sorta went through the motions. This time, it ended with a kiss on top of my head. That was a first.

A pesky little fly landed on my blanket. My grandfather seized his chance to, as he says, "bring that fly to his knees." He's the only person I know who has a fly swatter collection. When we visited Texas last year, I bought him one that was so massive, you could swat a piñata with it. Pops claims it's his prized possession.

As he focused on the annoying insect—who, at times, seemed to switch into stealth mode—he spoke like he was the commander of a military operation. "Don't worry, Nicholas. I'll nab this little bugger." The fly tried to escape, but Pops was the victor. Anyway, I hate when flies land on me, so I was glad he nailed it.

I heard the door slam and looked at the clock. My brother was home. He slid his backpack across the floor like he did every day and tossed his car keys into the little dish on the counter. Ever since Eddie got his driver's license, he thinks he's a big shot. "Aww...poor baby. Nicky, are you sicky?" Do all teenagers harass their younger brothers?

Mom gave him a look that said he'd better knock it off. "Eddie...Nick just got home from the doctor's office. He passed out in school today."

He snarled at my mom like he was defending his honor. "How was I supposed to know that?"

In an irritated whisper Mom said, "I didn't say you were *supposed* to know that...but you know now, so go say something encouraging to him." She was in no mood. It doesn't happen often, but when Mom gets that way, we clear the area.

Eddie strolled over like it was all his idea.

Grandma grumbled at the TV. "Look at that purple hair. What on earth was she thinking?"

Eddie loved to tease her. "I'm getting blue streaks in my hair next week...I'll save some of the dye for you." He leaned in for a Gram hug.

"Your mom might have a thing or two to say about that."

Then he turned to me. "Baby bro...are you really sick or faking it?" He knows I hate when he calls me anything even close to a baby, but he actually looked a little concerned. I guess Mom's worrying was contagious. "What happened?" I rolled my eyes back and dropped my bent arm to show I fainted, and that's right about when the phone rang.

I heard Mom say, "Yes, Dr. Katz. Thanks for getting back to me so quickly." Then she got a look on her face that reminded me of when she found out my other grandma died. I heard things like "Okay, I understand" and "Where do we check in?"

My grandfather walked over to her and put his hand on her shoulder. When she hung up the phone, he asked, "What did he say?"

"He wants me to take Nick to the pediatric hospital as soon as possible. He made arrangements for additional tests." *Whatever this is, it doesn't sound good.* Mom left Dad a message on his cell and before I knew it, we were back in the car and headed to the hospital. No lasagna for me.

CHAPTER FOUR

"I know it is wet
and the sun is not sunny,
but we can have lots
of good fun that is funny."
—DR. SEUSS

My very first wheelchair ride had happened earlier that day at school, and there I sat, hours later, taking my second ride, this time down the hallway of a hospital, heading for my assigned room. Someone took the time to put pictures on the walls, but they were boring. It all looked a little creepy to me.

A lot happened between nine o'clock in the morning and three in the afternoon, and I was already sick and tired of all the pokes and tests. My mom was shocked when Dr. Katz met us at the emergency department.

He rattled off a list to the other doctor of things he'd already checked at his office. Next, we wheeled into a room with a "Radiology" sign on the door. I had to put on a lead apron so I didn't catch any radiation from the X-ray. In another room, a lady squirted warm slimy stuff on my stomach and moved a wand around in it to look inside my body. I tried to catch a glimpse, but nothing looked familiar.

After Dr. Katz officially admitted me to the hospital, he got to leave...Mom and I, on the other hand, were stuck there. At least I had a room all to myself with a TV, a chair and a huge window. I could see the main parking lot when I looked down. It was jammed with cars. There was a tall, rectangular table near my bed that rolled around. The best part was the bed moved up and down if I pressed the right buttons. I definitely wanted to play with that later when I had more energy.

A nurse who looked way serious walked into my room. "Good afternoon, young man. I'm Noreen." She handed me what looked like one of the old sheets we have in a closet at home. "Your mom can help you get into this gown." A *gown? Sheesh.* "I'll be in and out checking your blood pressure and temperature and using this little gadget." She clipped it onto my finger. "It measures the oxygen in your blood." I guess she didn't realize the other nurse had just done all that stuff at Dr. Katz's office. She called it my *vitals.* "The doctor asked for something else...a urine sample." She grabbed a cup from the bathroom and said, "You'll need to pee in this container."

Here we go again. I looked at my mom and whined, "I already peed in a cup once today. How much of that stuff do they need, 'cause it doesn't really want to come out anyway."

"You'll be fine, honey. Just do the best you can. Even if it's a small sample." My mom glanced at the nurse, looking for backup.

Noreen chimed in, "Just hold it and go." She was matter-of-fact about everything. *No Nonsense Noreen…Triple-N.*

I took care of business, making sure to follow directions. *Done.* Triple-N took my sample and exited, stage left.

Mom fixed my blankets again. "You've been having trouble going to the bathroom? You said it didn't want to come out?"

"Sometimes…"

"You never mentioned that."

"I thought it was just that one time, but it keeps happening."

"Hmmm." Mom had a faraway look.

In came a guy to take more of my blood. I figured he must know Viola.

Mom tried to make me laugh. "You're getting to be a pro…second blood draw in one day." *I'd rather be a baseball pro.*

"I hope they know what they're doing. I mean…I don't want to run low on blood."

"Don't worry…you have several pints, Nick. Besides,

your body will replace that blood in no time." *Whew.*

I played around with the remote, trying to turn on the TV. I landed on a good channel just as a different nurse showed up. "Hi there, Nick. I'm Desti. I'll be your BFF and favorite nurse during your stay in our beautiful establishment." BFF? *Okie-dokie.* "Let's get you hooked up to some fluids that will flow right into your veins. You won't even have to use a straw." She was the exact opposite of Triple-N. "You'll feel a little pinch on the back of your hand as I get this IV going." *Pinches. Pokes. Let's call it like it is...torture.* It felt like she jabbed me with a pencil. "I know...that might not have been the best experience you've ever had, but I promise...this stuff will eventually make you feel better than a tall drink of—she looked at Mom and asked, "What's his favorite drink?"

"He's a Pepsi fanatic." I had to agree with her.

"Okay...well, use your imagination...this will make you feel better than even an ice-cold Pepsi Cola would." She winked. *Kind of doubt it.*

She pressed on my legs and arms—I think she noticed the puffiness Dr. Katz had mentioned earlier that day—then she listened to my heart. "When you're feeling better, I'll roll a game console into your room."

"I'm starting to wonder if I'll *ever* feel better, but that would definitely help. Thanks."

"You betcha...whatever you need, sweetheart."

Just as Desti was about to leave, my stomach started feeling like it did when I rode the Tumbler at the Clark County Fair...and that did not end well for the kid sitting next to me. Desti couldn't get the bucket fast enough. I got sick all over the place. *Yuck.* It wouldn't have been so bad if she'd acted at least a *little* mean. "None of this is your fault, sweetie. Let's get you cleaned up." Delightful Desti. Nurses must have to take a course in being kind to sick kids. She probably got an A+ in that.

I went into the bathroom to change that weird gown. The least they could do is put buttons on those things. When I came out, my sheets were already changed like nothing happened. Triple-N must've stepped in to help.

I climbed back into bed, and Mom fluffed my pillows. I had just rolled over when I heard, "Hey, partner!"

I couldn't believe it. "Dad!"

He gave Mom a quick kiss on the cheek, and she said, "I thought your flight wouldn't arrive until later this evening?"

Dad looked like he'd just run a marathon. "I caught a standby flight." I noticed a tear in his eye, something I'd never seen before.

He pulled me up to his chest. "And you...let me squeeze the stuffins' outta ya." His gigantic hugs always made me feel safe. "I'm relieved to finally be here," he said as he ruffled my hair.

"You don't know the half of it, Dad. This has been one cra-zeee day."

"Oh yeah?...well I considered banging on the

cockpit door and telling the pilot to step on it." Dad grinned. "It was tough hearing about all this long distance. What's the latest?"

"Well, let's just say I have lots of material for my 'Most Embarrassing Moment Ever' essay." We both giggled a little, even though there was nothing funny about any of it. I guess we were just happy to see each other.

I didn't have it in me to go through the entire saga, but I gave him some highlights. "I just now got sick and the nurse cleaned it up." Dad made a face like he was glad he didn't have that job. "That's not all. A different lady spread cold, slimy gel all over my stomach and moved a wand around in it. She said she was looking at my kidneys, but I told her I was pretty sure I didn't have any."

"That was probably an ultrasound...everybody has kidneys, son. They're some of our vital organs. Didn't they teach you that in school?"

"I might have heard a thing or two about kidneys." Small lie. I just didn't want to sound stupid.

"They're pretty important. In fact, you have two of them—"

Mom interrupted, "I hate to break this up, but Nick, will you be okay for a few minutes while your dad and I walk down to the cafeteria? We won't be long." I was pretty sure she just wanted to talk privately to Dad about the whole ordeal.

"That's fine. Leave the door open when you go." I wanted to check out the commotion in the hallway. I thought I heard people yelling "Slow down!" Kind of strange for a hospital.

I was pretty shocked when, as they were leaving, I clearly saw that I wasn't imagining things. A boy in a wheelchair flew past my room at breakneck speed.

Dad said, "Whoa...where's he off to?"

"I don't know, but I'll bet he's gonna get in trouble." *Whoosh*...he blew by again. He must've been practicing for the Wheelchair Olympics. Good thing our wing of the hospital was pretty much deserted.

All of a sudden, his brakes squealed. I heard him holler, "Want a visitor?" almost like he was talking to me. *Wait a minute...he IS...*

"Uh...sure...I guess." I'll admit I was a little curious.

He whipped through my doorway, and the first thing I noticed was his blond hair. It wasn't messy or anything...just really long. *Doesn't that get in his way?* He reminded me of the surfers I'd seen on the California beaches.

"What are you in for?" He had a smile on his face, but his question still took me by surprise. As far as I knew, I wasn't in prison. His face looked familiar...kind of like the kid on the First Ward baseball team who hit a homer against me the last time I pitched. That kid had long hair too, but he pulled it back in a ponytail.

I looked at him and said, "I just got here today, so I don't really know what's wrong yet. They're doing tests to figure it out." I didn't wanna go into the whole drama about how I passed out in school and all that. "How 'bout you?"

"I have stomach problems once in a while." He wheeled over to the window and pretended to wave to the people in the parking lot. "I've been to this hospital so many times that I make rounds…like the doctors do. This place gets sooo boring after a while." He looked around the room, casing the place. I couldn't believe it when he hopped out of his wheelchair and walked over to check out the gaming system. "Cool…how'd you score this?"

"Dunno. A nurse wheeled it in."

"Yeah, that must've been Desti. She's the best nurse." *Yep. Delightful Desti.*

"Dude…doesn't it hurt to walk? I mean, I figured you couldn't even stand up since you're riding around in that chair."

He roared with laughter. *Doesn't take much to amuse him.* "I totally get the confusion," he said as he composed himself enough to speak, "but I'm fine. The nice nurses leave it near my doorway 'cause they know I like to cruise the halls." He chuckled a little when he explained, "They said it's okay to use as long as I don't go too fast or wreck into anybody."

I cracked up. "No offense, but you flew by my doorway like a racer in the Indy 500."

"As long as they don't catch me, I'm good to go." He was a fugitive on the run. "And, as soon as you get more energy, I'll let you take this chair for a spin."

"By the way, what's your name?"

"I'm Charlie. What's yours?"

"Nick. Roll by anytime."

"Later, dude." He almost clipped a nurse as he wheeled out of my room.

Meeting Charlie made me think about the kids at school. I'd already missed an entire week before I passed out, and since I'd landed in the hospital, I had no clue when I'd get back. I'd lose my turn to pitch in kickball for sure. When they skip you, it doesn't come around again for at least a month. Molly invented that rule.

Was that really just this morning when I collapsed in school? Wow...longest day ever. Later on, Dad went home and Mom slept on the not-so-comfy-looking chair in the corner of my hospital room. As soon as the night nurse shut off the light, I conked out. She woke me up a bunch of times to take my vitals, but I was so tired, I always fell back asleep instantly.

CHAPTER FIVE

"If you keep your eyes
open enough,
Oh, the stuff you will learn..."
—DR. SEUSS

Before I even had one eye all the way open, the door swung back and hit the wall. I figured it was Charlie paying me another visit, but instead, a tall man with a red ball stuck to his nose rolled in. And I do mean *rolled*. He was on a skateboard and wore a white coat like Dr. Katz. I glanced over at my parents; they looked just as confused as I was.

He flashed a toothy smile. "Good morning, Cicero family! I'm Dr. Dave."

We'd been waiting for him since I got admitted. "You finally made it!"

Mom gave me one of her *you better zip it* stares and snapped, "Nicholas!"

"Sorry...it's just that I thought maybe he forgot about us."

"Rest assured...I would never forget about you." The doctor reached for my hand to shake it when...*swoosh!*...I got hit with a cold blast of water.

"Hey! What was that about?" It squirted out of his tie and right onto my face! *Too bad I don't have a couple water balloons handy. This would be war.*

"Oh, boy. I see nobody spilled the beans about me. Sometimes the nurses give kids hints that I'm a bit of a practical joker." He pretended to hide behind his loaded tie.

I wiped off my face between smiles. "You got me good, Dr. Dave!"

"I sure did," he said. "It wouldn't have been as effective if you knew it was coming, right?" He wiggled his eyebrows up and down. "Now consider yourself warned about my sneaky ways."

He turned to shake my dad's hand, but Dad jumped back like, *Hey buster, you better not be squirting me with that tie.*

The doctor laughed out loud and said, "But seriously, folks...when I'm not acting like a clown, I'm a nephrologist."

"Nef-rall-o-what?" I asked.

"It's a bit tough to pronounce, so just know that I'm your kidney doctor. I fix kidneys that don't work right anymore."

What's up with all this kidney talk? "I don't want to seem rude again, but you might have the wrong room 'cause my kidneys aren't broken."

"Is your name Nick?"

"Yeah, but—"

"Then I'm pretty sure I have the right room." He smiled at my parents as he took off his clown nose and flipped his loaded tie around to the back of his shirt.

"Before we talk more about why this is the right room, let me take a quick look at you, Nicholas." He put his skateboard in the corner, walked back to my bed and pushed down the railing. First, a light in my eyes and ears. Then squeezes on the legs and arms. But it was that big stomach press that got me. *Whoa! Probably shouldn't make a move like that, Doc.* He used a stethoscope to listen to my heart and lungs. He clearly wasn't in clown mode anymore.

Apparently, it was time to get real. "Okay, Nick...do you prefer Nick or Nicholas?"

"Most people call me Nick."

He leaned near my bed, not only talking to me, but my parents too. "Most of us are born with two kidneys." *I guess Dad was right about that.* "You never notice them inside you because they hide out in your back area." I reached around to press on my back, but I couldn't feel any kidneys. He kept talking. "When you need to pee, you can thank your kidneys. They make that urine." He lifted the rail back up on my bed and grabbed a seat. I guess he planned to stay a while. "Ever eat kidney beans?"

"Only if Mom forces me...or bribes me." She nodded her head in total agreement.

Dr. Dave chuckled, "Those beans you hate got that name because they're shaped like human kidneys. The ones in your body are about as big as your fists." He popped up off the stool and held up two fists like he was ready to fight. *This guy's a joker.* "Lots of blood flows in our bodies, and the kidneys clean that blood. They're like two mini washing machines that not only filter your blood, but also make you urinate, keep your bones healthy, and balance your body. They even help you grow taller."

"I guess my kidneys didn't do too great in that department. My family members are all skyscrapers, but I didn't inherit that gene."

"That's possible." Dr. Dave sat down on the stool and looked back and forth at the three of us as he talked. "So, here's the thing. There are two issues we need to discuss. First, you were born with a pair of kidneys like most people, but only one has worked for all of your ten years."

"What?" Dad looked stunned. "We had no idea."

"There's no way you could've known, Mr. Cicero, unless Nick had an ultrasound done for some reason."

"I just had one done yesterday." *I swear I still have some of that slimy stuff on me.*

"You sure did. I'm the one who's been looking at the results of all those tests we ran on you. Anyway, when the functioning kidney did its job, it cleaned your blood. It kept the helpful stuff and got rid of the poisons, also known as toxins, whenever you urinated." *Hey...A.K.A...he's using my lingo.*

Dr. Dave looked right at me and said, "Lately, I hear you've been feeling pretty lousy."

"Uh, yeah, you could say that." *Like I said, having the flu sucks.*

"That leads me to the second issue: The kidney that previously worked decided to start shutting down."

Mom gasped. Dad walked over and put his arm around her. She said, "Wait a minute, Doctor. Are you saying *neither* of Nick's kidneys works?" Seemed she was about to lose it.

"Yes, unfortunately, that is what I'm saying. Nick, your body is an amazing machine, and it knows that bad stuff needs someplace to go. That's why you feel sick and why you vomited."

I had to fight back a lump in my throat; it was my kidneys that sucked. "Wow," I said, almost to myself. "I thought I had the flu." I glanced over at my father. There were those tears again.

He questioned the doctor, "How did this happen?"

Dr. Dave directed his kind eyes toward my parents. "Unfortunately, sometimes we just don't have an explanation for why things happen the way they do."

I didn't give them a chance to respond. "Okay, so I have *two* broken kidneys?"

"I'm afraid so, Nick." Dr. Dave looked concerned. *I think I liked him better when he squirted me with his tie.* "And kidneys are just as important to your body as your heart, your lungs, or any other major organ inside you, so we need to fix this."

"We're listening, Doc. What can we do?" *That's right, Dad. Let's figure this out fast and get the heck out of here.*

Dr. Dave said, "Let's take it one step at a time. We'll start preparations for you to receive dialysis right away. That's a treatment that takes over for your kidneys when they aren't working properly."

"I've certainly heard of dialysis," Mom looked a little sick herself, "but clearly we have a lot to learn."

My dad reached for her hand. "Maur...we'll get through this. Like the doc said...a step at a time."

Dr. Dave stood up. "That's right...It'll overwhelm you if you let it. That's why we have an entire team of people who'll be in your corner. One of them will be in shortly to explain more about dialysis and answer any questions you might have."

"I'm sure we'll have plenty." Mom gave a half smile, but she wasn't looking even *a quarter* happy.

"In order for you to have dialysis after you get home, Nick, we're going to have a surgeon insert a small, soft tube called a catheter in your stomach."

"I'm going under the knife?"

"Minor surgery. We'll schedule it as soon as we can."

Mom wanted reassurance. "Please tell me it's nothing to worry about."

"Not at all. After a couple weeks, the area will heal,

and he'll be ready to use the catheter to connect to the home dialysis machine." I got the feeling my zany doctor hated this part of his job. He looked tired, and it was only nine in the morning. "In the meantime, you'll get dialysis here in the hospital."

Dad chimed in, "I'm glad we have a team to help us figure all of this out."

"Absolutely. We'll be here when you need us. In the meantime, Nick, watch your diet...eat what our dieticians tell you to eat.

Dr. Dave snatched up his skateboard. "I gave you folks a lot to digest. So Nick, try to get some rest. I'll stop back tonight on my rounds, and we can talk more then."

And to think, yesterday morning all I had to worry about was putting up with Molly and her BS.

CHAPTER SIX

"Think left and think right
and think low and think high.
Oh, the things you can think up
if only you try!"
—DR. SEUSS

The next couple days were a whirlwind; the catheter went in, and it was almost like a part of my body now. They said I'd need another surgery eventually to get rid of it. The area around it was kind of sore, but the nurse said that was temporary. My fourth day of dialysis—it wasn't as bad as I thought it would be. My fourth day of hospital food—it was *worse* than I thought it would be. Most of the things I liked to eat were banned. The days of sugary cereal were gone. Mom didn't mind the less sugar part, but she shared my grief about the rest of it. Now, breakfast was no-salt scrambled eggs or apple oatmeal. *Gross.* Lunch usually included a hamburger or a chicken pattie and a slice of tomato. Chips were out. Carrots and celery were in. *Wonder what's on the menu for dinner tonight?* I never liked a single thing on the tray anyway, but it was all I had to look forward to.

Irene, my dietician, said the same thing over and over again: "Your kidney shouldn't work any harder than it needs to." The list was long. No peanut butter. No salt. No fast food. I was allowed to have jelly on my toast. Big deal. I hate jelly. What I do like is fiery chips, but those were vetoed too. And, it wasn't just food that was off limits. I couldn't gulp down Pepsi either. Talk about torture. In fact, I had to measure how much of *any* liquid I drank, 'cause I could only have a certain amount of fluids. *Hope I don't dry up.*

What I wanted most was to be out of the hospital and back in my own bed. The medicine made me feel better, but I kept wondering...Why me? Of all the kids in the world, why did I have to be the one with two broken kidneys? And one of them never worked at all. *What a ripoff.*

Time dragged on. For eleven days in a row, I waited for Dr. Dave to make his before-dinner rounds. He always had some kind of trick up his sleeve. Charlie and I even dreamed up a few of our own once in a while, but we were no match for Dr. Dave. Years of practice, I guess.

After nearly two weeks of no phone calls, a louder-than-usual ringtone blasted from my cell phone, breaking the silence. I jumped a mile, then lurched to answer it.

"Hey, Nick." It was Sneezy on the other end. "We were hoping you'd answer. Bam's with me."

"Hi, George. I didn't expect a phone call! Did you guys just get home from school?"

Sam chimed in, "Yep...we're playing video games and wondering when you're coming back." Sam's addicted to the NFL video game. "Seems like you've been gone forever!"

So much happened, and it did seem like I'd been out of school for a long time. "I'm supposed to go home tomorrow, then back to school Monday."

"Awesome!" said George. "You haven't missed much...except...we asked Mr. Vanasco if there'd be a fifth grade dance this year. He said yes...at the Valentine's Day Festival."

"Awesome," I said. "It's a long way off, but it's going to be epic."

Sam teased, "Think you'll ask Caroline to dance?" They razzed me a bit 'cause they knew about my little crush.

"What?! No way...I can barely even spit out a hello when she's around." We all cracked up thinking about that, but it was true. I'd probably chicken out and not even speak to her, let alone ask her to dance. What if I knocked that big barrette thingy out of her curly brown hair? Plus, if they played a slow song, we'd have to touch each other...*Sheesh*.

"Oh yeah...and we read through *Romeo and Juliet* again. Bam has the Romeo part wrapped up." George was excited for him.

"Really? I thought Miss T wasn't assigning parts yet."

"She isn't, but my money's on him for gettin' it. Just a matter of time."

Bam didn't deny wanting to be Romeo. "What about you, Nick? Do you wanna be one of the actors...or work behind the scenes?"

"I do like swords, so I could be one of the sword fighters. Maybe Mercutio. He has some funny lines." My mind drifted back to Caroline. "So who do you think will be Juliet? I'm thinkin' Caroline would be perfect for that part."

"Ooooo...there you go again...you love her..." Bam enjoyed teasing me.

"I don't *love* her. I *like* her. Just as a friend though. There's nothing mushy about it." *Doubt I'd admit to it anyway.*

"It's good to have lots of friends, even girls." *Thanks for the save, Sneezy.*

"Well guys, I hear my doctor rambling down the hall on his skateboard."

Sam was impressed. "On a skateboard? No way!"

"I know...pretty crazy, right? Thanks for calling. Means a lot."

They both yelled, "Get better soon!" at the same time.

I could tell they really meant it. The line went dead just as Mom and Dad walked into my room.

I started telling them about my surprise phone call, but Dr. Dave blew in just then without stopping, beeping his red nose. "Good afternoon, Ciceros!" For a split second I thought he would land on my bed. *Slow it down, Dr. Dave!* "I hope you don't mind...I brought a helper with me today."

I looked up and saw a second red nose peeking around the corner—this time attached to my best friend. "What? How did you get in here?" D grinned from ear to ear.

"Surprise!" Dr. Dave must have slipped Diego one of his noses. "I'll bet you didn't expect to see me today. And...I brought you cards from the class."

"Really? They made me cards?"

"Sure did. There's a bunch of them. My mom was coming here to visit her friend, so I told the teacher I could be the delivery boy."

"I just hung up the phone with Bam and Sneezy!" I felt happy for the first time in a while.

Mom said, "So nice they called...and we thought a friendly face might cheer you up a little." She was right about that.

I wondered if the kids even *knew* I was in the hospital, but I found out the answer to that. "*Gracias*, Diego! And thank the rest of the class, too."

"Mr. and Mrs. Cicero, how 'bout we grab a cup of coffee while these two catch up?"

"Sounds great." It was nice to see Mom smile again.

As soon as they left the room, Diego hijacked the stethoscope that Desti left on my table. "You better hope Nurse Desti doesn't catch you touching that." *He would definitely get along well with Charlie.*

"Why? Is she mean?" Diego must've imagined a nurse as tough as our last substitute teacher.

I thought about everything Desti had done for me since I arrived. "Nah…actually, she left that for me to play with 'cause it's her spare. You'd like her. She snorts when she laughs, just like you."

Diego leaned right in to listen to my heart. I think he actually believed he was a doctor for a second. "Yep. Your heart is beating all right." He had no trouble amusing himself.

"It better be. Let me hear *your* heart now…" D handed me the stethoscope. I used a wipe from the pack on my table to clean his ear wax off the ends. *Disgusting.* "Yours is ticking too."

The big envelope stuffed with cards piqued my curiosity. "Okay, let's see what you brought me."

He dumped them on my sheets and said, "Every single kid in class made you one."

There were so many cards that a few of them tumbled off the bed, but Diego caught them mid-air. They all wrote, "Get well, Nick." Even Molly. She actually said something half nice. "We miss you." *That's debatable, but it's the thought that counts.*

We heard one of the nurses yell at Charlie to slow down. Diego flashed his eyes at me through his ebony glasses. He craned his neck to see the action in the hallway, so I filled him in on my frequent visitor. "Dude, I met this kid here named Charlie. He gets to ride a wheelchair around for fun."

D's wheels were spinning. "No way! I want to try that."

Just then, Charlie made a quick turn into my room and barreled right up to the bed. "Whoa...didn't know anyone else was in here."

Diego laughed his head off. "You're pretty good with that hunk of metal. I'll bet it's not easy to steer."

I could tell Charlie appreciated the fact that D was loving his escapades. "Charlie, this is my best friend from school—he's my neighbor too—Diego."

Charlie gave D a little nod. "How'd you get past the nurses?"

"Nick's mom worked it out with the doctor."

Charlie said, "She *must've* pulled some strings, 'cause that's no easy feat."

"Really?" I said. *Score one for Mom.*

He spun the wheelchair in the other direction. "I better get back to my room before they send a search party. I'm getting out today. Hope you do too, Nick."

Diego offered, "Need some help with that? I think I'd be a pretty good driver."

I chimed in, "Yeah, right. I can just picture you two now...cutting loose, racing down the halls." I shook my head.

Charlie lit up. "Hey! Good idea!" He rolled back toward my bed and said, "Let's do it!"

I know he gets bored here, but…"I thought you had to get back to your room. Besides, I was just kidding!" I sure didn't want that idea pinned on me.

You don't have to twist Diego's arm…he's up for anything. "I'm in. C'mon, Nick. A wheelchair race would be awesome."

Charlie's eyes actually twinkled. "I know right where they park the extra wheelchairs. Come with me, Diego." *Uh-oh.*

They took off, and I lay there wondering how long Dr. Dave and my parents would stay in the cafeteria. *Puh-leeze…drink an extra cup of coffee.*

Two wheelchairs bounced off the walls and into my room. "Okay, Nick. You can't miss this." Charlie grabbed my IV stand. "We'll help you move this thingamajig over by the door so you can watch our race." *Great…now I'm an accessory to this bad idea.* "Plus, you need to blow the start whistle. Don't worry…it won't take long."

"I don't know about this, guys." Charlie forged ahead like he didn't even hear me. Before I had a chance to talk them out of it, I was the official race starter, an accomplice. I cringed.

I stood in the doorway as they headed to the other end of the hall. Thankfully, the coast was clear. I yelled in the loudest voice I could muster up, "On your mark…get set…go!"

D and Charlie pushed on those wheels with all their might. You'd have thought the prize was a million dollars. First, Charlie was in the lead, but then he almost ran into a linen cart, so Diego edged in front of him. As they neared the finish line, Charlie gave it everything he had. He didn't even notice Dr. Dave and my parents as they rounded the corner. *Busted.*

"I'm the victor!" Charlie screamed, throwing his hands up in the air. He obviously didn't realize he'd been caught red-handed.

Diego didn't notice either, and he was too excited to care who won or lost. "When that lady came out of her room, you actually tipped on two wheels trying to miss her."

My mom almost fainted when she saw me standing in the doorway, far from the bed, leaning on my IV pole. "Nicholas!" She was not amused, to say the least. None of the adults were.

Dad blurted out, "Boys! What on earth is going on?! This is a hospital with sick people who need their rest."

Nurse Desti must've seen at least the tail end of the action, 'cause she ran into the room right after my parents. She gave Charlie one of those *Are you kidding me?* looks. "I'm wheeling you back to your room, Mister Charles." *She likes him, so hopefully he won't get in too much trouble, but his wheelchair-riding days are probably over.*

As she whisked him away, our ring leader glanced back, "Good race, Diego."

D replied, "*Adiós,* Charlie." We tried to hold it in...no luck...the three of us burst out laughing. Mom rushed me back to bed, but she yanked on that IV so hard she almost ripped it out of my arm. "Don't ever pull a stunt like that again." *Good thing I'm sick or I'd be grounded this week for sure.*

Dr. Dave disappeared and Dad said, "You boys are lucky you didn't break anything, including your bones...or worse yet, someone else's bones. We're going to say a quick hello to Diego's mom, so you have about five more minutes together. Behave!"

When they were out of sight, D let out one of his snorty giggles that made his ebonies slide down his nose, "At least it's not totally boring here."

"True." *Not anymore.*

"When can you blow this popcorn stand?" Everything always seemed so simple to Diego.

"I'm supposed to go home tomorrow, then back to school on Monday, but I think I might just say I'm not ready yet."

"Why would you do that?" Diego's face dropped. "The kids can't wait to see you! Are you sick?"

I raised my eyebrows. *Duh, I'm in a hospital.*

"You know what I mean," he said, clearly frustrated with me. "Are you too sick for school?"

"No, it's just that I feel weird about going back after everything that happened. The other kids might...never mind. I just don't want to go yet." *And I don't want to talk about it.*

"Don't worry...I told them you're not contagious." Diego snatched a disposable mask from the box on the wall. He covered his nose and mouth with it, held his hand on his throat and coughed like he was being choked by disease. "Besides, the Matts made up a new dance just for you. You gotta go!" Mattie Fire and Mattie Ice were cousins who were in our class in fourth grade, but they ended up with a different teacher for fifth. They're practically professional dancers.

D tossed his mask in the trash can, then walked over to play with the buttons on my bed. He explored more of that room in five minutes than I had in two weeks.

"They made up a dance just for me?" *All kinds of surprises today.* "Well...I don't know. I might get tired...and I can't really play kickball...definitely not football...and I have to eat weird stuff now. You won't believe the food that's off limits to me." The truth is, I was just afraid everyone would think I was strange 'cause I passed out that day and had a tube in my stomach. They might treat me like *the sick kid* instead of the kinda cool Nick I was when I left.

Diego blurted out, "Brainstorm! Remember when we made up that famous dance that nobody in the world could copy?"

Slight exaggeration. "Yeah."

"Let's walk onto the playground Monday doing that dance, acting like we own the place. I'll be right there with you. Maybe we could have a dance-off with the cousins!"

"Yeah...maybe..." My best friend could always talk me into stuff. "I don't know about a dance-off though. Those *primos* would kick our butts." We cracked up thinking of our dance steps compared to the moves of Mattie Fire and Mattie Ice.

We wrapped up our plan, and D's mom showed up to take him home. He was about to leave when I noticed Desti's stethoscope around his neck. "Hey, Doctor Diego...aren't you forgetting something?"

"Okay, okay. Just teasing," he laughed. "Do they sell these things in the gift shop? It's pretty cool."

I rolled my eyes. "I doubt it."

"I'll be at your house Monday morning, bright and early, Nick. Dress the part...hat and shades."

I gave him a thumbs-up. *Looks like I'll be dancing my way back into fifth grade Monday.*

CHAPTER SEVEN

"Take every chance.
Drop every fear."
—Dr. Seuss

I was finally out of the hospital. Back in my own bed. Nobody needed to wheel me anywhere or take my blood pressure. Charlie checked out before I had a chance to say goodbye or get his phone number. He sure made being on the inside more bearable.

Velcro licked my face even more than usual. I'm pretty sure he missed our daily walks. I scratched behind his ears and apologized. "Velcro, you might have to wait a few days before we start our walks again." He seemed content that I was back to scratching his ears at least.

Mary Eileen, a nurse from our team, came to our house to train Mom, Dad and me on how to do peritoneal dialysis. We did a different kind in the hospital, but since I got my catheter in, I could do this type at home while I slept. She had to teach me how to *say* it. PEH-rih-tuh-NEE-ul. It's called PD for short, which is a whole lot easier to remember. She said the machine was called a cycler. I liked her right away because she told me to call her Mary I for short.

"But don't call me Mary Nose, like my brothers did when we were growing up." She winked. I guess she heard I like to give out nicknames. She taught Gram and Pops how to do dialysis too, just in case my parents needed backup.

The cycler got connected to my catheter every night like clockwork. It felt like I was on a leash. Velcro must've thought he was on a leash too, 'cause he never left my side. Mom slept on a cot in my bedroom for the entire first week. I guess she wanted to make sure I was okay. I have to admit...I was glad. Eventually, my parents became pros at firing up that cycler.

I only had the weekend to rest up before heading back to school on Monday. My morning routine now included shots—the one I needed every day to help me grow and the one I got twice a week to help me make blood. Dr. Dave explained why I was getting them and how my kidneys weren't telling my bone marrow to make blood cells. I had no clue all that stuff happened inside my body every day. Of course, I had to swallow five thousand pills too. Exaggeration? Maybe. But it was a lot to choke down. And, just so you know, I still hate shots.

Monday morning finally arrived, and Mom sounded as nervous as I felt. "Nick, are you ready up there?"

"Almost." I gave myself a hard look in the mirror. I put on an extra-long shirt so it wouldn't slide up and expose my catheter tube. *Will anybody notice this tube in my stomach?* I wore the orange and navy plaid fedora I got for my birthday last year. Chicago Bears' colors. It amped up my confidence level for sure. Hands down, it was the coolest thing in my closet. That, along with my new prescription sunglasses, and I looked good, if I do say so myself.

Mom yelled up again, "Diego's waiting!" As I came down the stairs, he gave me a thumbs-up. He wore his shades and hat too.

He slid to the right in a little dance step, spun around, then flashed his trademark smile. "*Vámonos!*"

"Yep, let's hit the road." I felt better once D was there.

Before I even opened the door, Mom reminded me for the hundredth time, "I'm just around the corner if you need me today."

"I know that, and I promise, I'm going to be fine." I hugged her, even though D was looking. She needed it.

"Have a good day, boys. Don't let him overdo it today, Diego."

"Okay, Mrs. C."

We walked down the street toward George E. Harris like we'd done loads of times before. As we turned the corner toward the school, butterflies flew around, full throttle, in my stomach. Then Diego sang out, "Oh yea-a-a-a-h...he's back in action!" I felt a smile break out on my face. *I guess maybe I am.*

"Knock, knock."

Oh boy. Here we go. He loves those stupid jokes. "Who's there?" I always played along.

"Ketchup."

"Ketchup who?"

"Ketchup to me and I'll tell you." He took off running all the way to the playground. I tried to keep up, but I decided to save some energy for our dance.

George was the first person I spotted. His face lit up when he saw me. "Hey, Nick, you're back! Looking pretty dapper with your lid and shades."

"Thanks, Sneeze. I'm glad to be here. To celebrate, Diego and I are gonna do our dance. You know the one...the only song we dance to." We both cracked up at that because it was so true.

"Awesome! I've got the music..." He cranked up the volume on his phone 'cause he was our usual DJ. Even if we weren't the best dancers on the planet, Diego and I definitely had more fun than anyone else on Earth while doing our little routine...we felt like rock stars for one bright, shining moment.

Sneezy was fired up. "Gather 'round, guys. Nick is back!" We broke into our dance as soon as the song started. We had our steps down, and everyone clapped along to the beat.

Two shoulder shakes to the right. Snap. Snap.

Two to the left. Stomp. Stomp.
Snap it up. Criss-cross.
Wave to the left. Wave to the right...

A crowd of kids—and even a couple playground monitors—started to form as the sound carried across the playground. We broke into our favorite part, *the sprinkler.* We found that move online. Just then, Mattie Fire and Mattie Ice jumped in. They have so much rhythm—dancing is their sport. It seems like they even *walk* to a drum beat. They take hip hop lessons three times a week with some famous guy who knows the Jabberwockeez, and it shows.

Mattie Ice said, "Welcome back, Nick. This one's for you." Diego high-fived me. Mattie Fire nodded at George to change the music, and we watched the cousins do their routine. The crowd hooted and hollered. I was relieved when they took over. I was too tired to have an actual dance off. I was out of breath after about thirty seconds. They were strong till the end. The day was off to a great start, and I wondered why I was afraid to face my fear of going back to school.

When the bell rang, we walked into the building, and Diego and I hung our fedoras on the coat hooks. I placed mine just right so the brim wouldn't get smashed, then I took my same old seat. Caroline turned around and whispered, "I love your hat..." She was about to say something else, but we had to stand for the Pledge of Allegiance.

Even though everything had changed with me, nothing had changed at school—math groups, word study, science...typical fifth-grade stuff. I had some work to catch up on, but nothing I couldn't handle. As if on cue, my stomach let out an embarrassing growl. It was time for lunch.

Just like before, whoever we followed into the row was who we had to sit by. I landed between Sneezy and Eli. Molly sat on the other side of George. I never understood why we couldn't sit across from each other. *Why is that such a big deal?*

I had a scary thought. *What if Mom packed me a no-salt ketchup sandwich?* No one would want to switch lunches with *me* for the "ten-second silent lunch trade." *I guess my days of trading food are over...at least for a while.* Once we all got seated, we swapped food we didn't want and replaced it with something better from someone else's lunch. Or at least, that was the goal. It didn't always work that way, but when it did, it was pretty slick—and a great way to unload a box of raisins. If Mr. Mike, the lunch monitor, had known about it, he would've nailed us for sure, but he never caught anyone. I had to look away when a bag of chips was in the rotation. *I wonder what would happen if I just ate one tiny little chip? I wish.*

Phew! Mom packed carrot sticks and hummus, no-salt crackers and a piece of watermelon. Kids wouldn't clamor to barter with me, but at least there was no sign of salt-free ketchup.

Funny, when I found out I had CKD—that's chronic kidney disease—I started noticing other people's food and how much nutrition they got from it. I was always on my computer checking things like how much phosphorus was in a container of yogurt or whether tangerines were low in sodium. I downloaded a bunch of apps Irene told me about to help me figure out what I could and couldn't eat. I didn't even know there were minerals in food before my CKD, and I definitely didn't realize they were such a big deal.

After the trade—at the exact same time Molly unwrapped her sandwich—George let out a series of sneezes that would make even the bravest run for cover.

"GEORGE!" The BS prez was not the least bit pleased about her sandwich getting sprayed.

Eli, the fact machine, immediately reported, "Sneezes travel about 100 miles per hour and send 100,000 germs into the air." I love how the professor keeps talking, even if no one's listening. "A lady from England set a world record sneezing 978 days straight." He definitely says what's on his mind, and I admire that.

"Sorry, Molly. I can't help it when I sneeze." George seemed embarrassed.

"Maybe not, but have you ever heard of sneezing into your elbow?!" Molly flipped her braided hair over her shoulder and pretended to sneeze into her arm as an example. *Oh, brother. What a know-it-all.*

"George doesn't have much time to react. Sneezing

is an automatic reflex that can't be stopped once it starts." *Tell her Eli.*

Molly glared at the prof, then blurted out, "Dear friend, talk not to me, for I'll not speak a word!" She'd obviously started memorizing some old English lines from *Romeo and Juliet*, 'cause she took those words straight from the script. When she said "I'll not speak a word," I hoped that meant she was done talking. *Definite bonus.*

We headed out to the playground, and I had a funny feeling something might happen to me out there. As soon as I walked onto the grassy area—WHAM! A soccer ball nailed me in the gut. I screamed and held onto my catheter like I was going to save it or something. The kids rushed over to see if I was okay.

Diego's face dropped. "Let's have the nurse check it out, Nick." Maybe he understood more than I thought.

Thankfully, Nurse Abby said everything looked normal with my tube. She had me stay in the health office until lunch was over. She even let Diego hang out there with me. *I hope this doesn't mean the play-ground's off limits now.*

I was glad we had art class and not PE that afternoon. I felt pretty worn out, but Dr. Dave said I should expect to drag a little since I'd spent nearly two weeks in the hospital.

At the end of the day, I wrote my homework down in my planner like I'd done twelve thousand times before and packed up to go home.

Diego and I usually raced each other most of the way, but I wasn't up for that yet, so we just walked.

He asked, "When can you spend the night again?"

"I have no idea, now that I'm chained to my cycler. At least I get to go to school and see everyone though." I felt sorry for myself because all my fun stuff seemed to be vanishing right before my eyes.

"Who ever heard of being *happy* to go to school?" Diego chuckled.

"Yeah, who ever heard of that?" *Just me.*

CHAPTER EIGHT

*"If things start happening,
don't worry, don't stew,
just go right along
and you'll start happening too."*
—DR. SEUSS

Kidney Schmidney. I think all this kidney stuff was harder on my parents than it was on me. Every once in a while they'd get into an argument about doing things with my cycler a certain way. I stayed out of it. No doubt it was tough with all they had to learn in order to help me.

I must've heard a jillion times, "Be sure to wash your hands before you touch your stomach or the dialysis equipment." A blaring alarm on my cycler went off whenever the tube got blocked. I guess I rolled over on it a lot and jammed it. It rarely woke me up. That's one advantage of being a sound sleeper. My parents would tell me about it the next day. No wonder they looked so tired. Mom said Velcro barked every single time the alarm rang. I guess he thought he was helping.

Kind of weird this PD stuff. I finally understood why the machine was called a cycler. It cycled the cleaning solution in and out of the lining of my belly. Mary I said, "Fill. Dwell. Drain. That's what your cycler does five times a night. It gets rid of those toxins."

I visited Dr. Dave for the gazillionth time. I learned something new. He said, "Did you know the big word for belly is *abdomen*? Stomachs are something different. They're for digesting food. The abdomen houses all those organs from your chest to your hip bones. The lining of your abdomen is called the peritoneum."

"Oh...now I get it. That's why they call it peritoneal dialysis."

"You're catching on, Nick."

"Maybe I'll be a kidney doctor someday like you. Then, when sick kids come to me, I'll know just how they feel."

Dr. Dave ruffled my hair. "The world needs more nephrologists. After all, there are loads of kids to squirt in the face." I gave him one of those looks like, *really, Doc?*

I'd only been getting dialysis for a few months, but it felt like a few years. The holidays came and went and thankfully, we kept very busy. I missed the candy that was usually in my stocking, but I got through it. We saw the team from the hospital so much they started to seem more like friends than doctors and nurses. One bright spot was that the numbers on my blood tests got better...and I even grew a half inch taller.

Life took on what Pops called a "new normal"...not just for me, but for my family. My parents not only fought about my cycler getting hooked up right, they also argued about money. They had no clue I was listening. All because of me and my defective kidneys.

Dad went on business trips again for his job, and Mom worked from home so she was there if I needed her. Then, one day, Dr. Dave said he'd like both my parents to be at the next appointment. We wondered what he needed to tell us. We soon found out.

Dr. Dave brought us into his office instead of the exam room. "I've always said we'd take this one step at a time, Nick..." *Oh boy. Here we go with more steps.* "You're getting a lot stronger, so we're at the point where we need to talk about getting you a new kidney. We'll continue with the dialysis until we find a match."

"How am I going to get another kidney? I've never seen a store for kidneys."

The doctor chuckled. "That would be handy, but it doesn't work that way. You'll need a kidney transplant."

"Is that kind of like when my grandmother transplants flowers from her yard to our yard?"

"It's very much like that. We have to get a kidney from another person that will be just right for your body. It can come to us in several different ways. First, we'll see if there's a compatible family member or friend who will donate one of their kidneys. Remember, people only need one functioning kidney, so most of us have a spare."

"I'll give him one of my kidneys!" Dad said.

"Could that work?" I asked. "After all, you only need one."

"We can certainly test you to see if that's possible, Mr. Cicero," said the doctor. "Family members top the list of good choices, but a lot goes into this decision. Again, a step at a time."

"But how would we get it from his body to mine?" I couldn't picture how this would happen.

"When the time comes, the surgeon will remove the donor's kidney from his or her body and put it into yours."

"So I'd go into an operating room again?" *Fantastic.*

"You sure would. This time, you'll fly to UCLA Medical Center in Los Angeles."

"Why would I go there?" *Hmm...maybe I can catch a Dodgers' game. Hope they play the Cubs.*

"It's the best match for location and your parents' insurance. And they're top-notch."

Dad said, "You were a real pro the last time you had an operation." *I don't know if I'd go that far, but I got through it.*

"What if nobody in my family can give me a kidney? One time, Eddie took the last piece of pizza right off my plate, so I'm pretty sure he's not parting with either of his kidneys."

The doctor chuckled. "You could get one from a deceased donor." *Is he saying what I think he's saying?* "Some people set it up to donate their organs when they die." *Yep, that's what I thought he was saying.* "UCLA will put you on a recipient list for that too. Then, if a kidney that matches yours becomes available, they'll call your parents, and you'll all find out about it quickly. Of course, either way, with a living donor or a deceased donor, the team at UCLA will want to meet all of you beforehand, so you can learn who they are and how they do things."

I said, "Mom and Dad are donating their organs when they die. That's why they have little red hearts on their driver's licenses."

"I'm doing that too, Nick. I wish more folks would. Glad to hear your parents told you kids their wishes. That's important." He gave my parents an approving smile.

I wondered why people agree to give their organs away after they die...maybe because part of them would sort of keep on living. *Pretty cool.* "Well," I said, "I sure hope more donors sign up soon." *From what I'm hearing...I need a kidney...and fast.*

That night, after I hooked up to the dialysis machine and finally drifted off to sleep, a dream woke me. I was laughing and playing football with my friends. It seemed so real. I was perfectly healthy. I lay there, awake...thinking about how my life had changed. For the first time, I felt the fluid moving in and out of my body from the dialysis. I stayed awake for a long time noticing that strange sensation. As weird as it was, it was keeping me alive.

CHAPTER NINE

"Don't give up! I believe in you all.
A person's a person, no matter how small."
—DR. SEUSS

On the drive home, Mom talked about everyone who might want to get tested to see if they'd be a match for me. She mentioned Pops and Grandma. Dr. Dave said they had to be in excellent health and not more than seventy years old. Pops looked pretty old to me, but he always says he's *as fit as a fiddle*. I guess that's good.

I walked into the house and immediately stretched out on the couch. A few minutes later...*Thump. Thud.* The backpack hit the wall, and the keys landed in the dish. Eddie was home. He talked to Mom in the kitchen. She filled him in on the latest news.

He picked up the whiteboard from the counter

and plopped himself down next to me on the couch. *Well, hello to you too, Ed.* He scribbled furiously on the whiteboard. Then he said, "Hey, little bro...what do you think of this?" He drew a boy holding up a sign that read, "Will work for kidney." Sometimes he can be funny. "Think he looks like you?" He manages to make me laugh at the craziest times.

"Wait, I've got a better one, Ed." I picked up a red marker and drew a picture of one big, fat, powerful kidney. I used a dark purple color to give it eyes, little arms and feet, and a face with a look that meant business. I added a blue mask and a blue cape—not the long, flowy kind like Superman wears—but it was just as cool. I put a big red "K" on the cape. I was on a roll. I mustered up my best superhero voice like they use in the movies..."Kidney Man to the rescue!"

"Hang on...you forgot one thing." Eddie drew two other kidneys next to my healthy one. "Those are your old kidneys. We can't forget those two little suckers." We both laughed out loud at that one. Then he said, "Nick Cicero—A.K.A. Kidney Man!"

"That's a good one, Ed! Finally, I have an awesome nickname, too." I decided I might even sign all my papers at school with my new alias. Miss Taylor wouldn't mind.

"Keep your eye on the prize..." is what Dr. Dave told me. Some days that was hard to do. Other days, I thought, *I got this.*

My parents and I returned from our first trip to UCLA. If I was lucky enough to get a kidney, the team there would do the transplant, so I had to go to California to get a bunch of tests done. They wanted to be sure I was mentally prepared—you know, up for the challenge. We did a lot of talking about it.

Doctor Dave kept in touch with the UCLA doctors. "They don't give kidneys to just anyone, Nick. But you and your family are ready to receive this gift when we find a match. You've passed all the tests that let us know you can handle the stress of it all. You really impressed the UCLA team."

I understood it was a gift, that's for sure. Still, it wasn't easy to understand the *why* of it all. I went from begging for a new video game to praying for a new kidney. Like Pops always says, "Life can turn on a dime." My body was tired, my mind was tired, and I was tired of chronic kidney disease. I wished I'd never heard those words.

I made a list of people who said they'd give me one of their kidneys if they jumped over all the hurdles—same blood type, good health, two working kidneys, not too old, not too young. I was surprised that so many people wanted to help. Mom and Dad would've been at the top of the list, but Mom had a different blood type than me, and Dad had high blood pressure. One of my brother's friends offered to give me a kidney, but he had diabetes, so he couldn't. He was too young anyway. Pretty nice of him though. Oh yeah...even Eddie said

I could absolutely have one of his. It's true he talked a big game, but I think he actually worried about me. Too bad Dr. Dave said he wasn't old enough. Neither were Diego and Katie. I decided to send thank you cards to everyone who either got tested or wanted to be. I didn't even complain about writing them like I normally do for birthday gifts.

When I found out someone wasn't a match, I crossed that name off my list. I hid the list way in the back of my dresser drawer because I didn't want my parents to know I kept track. They might think I was worried. That list shrunk each day, and every time I drew a line through another name, I felt devastated all over again. I tried to hide my feelings; I didn't want to bring everybody else down with me. *I'll have to find out if dogs can donate kidneys. I know Velcro wouldn't mind, and I'll bet he has kidneys too.*

For now, I waited. One thing that kept my mind off *the list* was our play at school. Can you believe I was actually excited to get to school? We were rereading *Romeo and Juliet* again and very close to assigning parts. My big worry was that I'd miss the tryouts because of a doctor's appointment. Now that would be a major letdown.

People Who Might Give Me a Kidney

~~Mom—wrong blood type~~

~~Dad—high blood pressure~~

Grandpa

~~Grandma—diabetes~~

~~Eddie's friend, Enrique—diabetes,~~
~~too young~~

~~Eddie—too young~~

~~Katie—too young~~

~~Diego—too young~~

Aunt Faith

~~Uncle Pat—diabetes~~

~~Dad's best friend Phil—overweight~~
(I might put him back on if his diet works)

Aunt Joyce

~~Uncle Don—had cancer~~

Uncle Bob

~~Mom's friend Jan—had cancer~~

~~A bunch of other relatives and friends—~~
a bunch of other reasons

Velcro???

Get a kidney from someone who died—
a deceased donor. (That one hurts.) ☹

CHAPTER TEN

"Why fit in when you
were born to stand out?"
—DR. SEUSS

My worst fear came true. My appointment with the nephrology team fell on the same day as tryouts for the play. Since those visits are tough to reschedule, I had to go. I couldn't get my mind off the auditions though. Miss Taylor drilled it into our heads. "If you don't show up, you don't get a part." To audition for a role, we had to memorize and recite part of a character's lines and deliver it with lots of expression. I had four of Mercutio's lines down pat. *I guess all that memorizing was for nothing.*

At my appointment, Dr. Dave told me an interesting fact. "You're pretty unique, Nick. There are approximately 74 million kids in the United States, and only about 800 get kidney transplants annually." *Not exactly the kind of list I wanted to top, Doc. I'd rather land a part in the play.*

The next morning, I moved like a turtle to the class line, and I had trouble even faking a smile. Molly stood front and center, of course. Everyone knew she'd changed her mind about playing Juliet. Instead, she decided to try out for Juliet's mother, Lady Capulet. Definitely more her style. She's a head taller than Caroline, so she just might get that part due to her height, if nothing else. "Hi, Nick." *There's that smirk.* "Too bad you missed auditions for the play."

I didn't say anything back to Molly. For once, I kept my mouth shut because I could see Caroline listening to our conversation. After we got into the classroom and heard the morning announcements, Caroline turned around and said, "Just ignore Molly. She thinks she's being funny." *Yep, she heard the whole thing.*

Immediately after I unloaded my backpack, Miss Taylor held the classroom microphone and said, "Mercutio! Where art thou?" She spoke in her best *Romeo and Juliet* accent and really laid on the old English. *Geez, talk about rubbing it in that somebody else got the Mercutio part.* "I do beseech thee, Mercutio, come hither." She looked straight at me. *Wait...Is she talking to me?* Caroline giggled and motioned me to go to the front of the class. "Nicholas, at our weekly meeting yesterday, the class voted to give you the part of Romeo's good friend, Mercutio, if you want it. What say you, kind sir?"

"Really?!" I couldn't believe my ears. I thought for sure I'd missed my chance. When I gave the teacher a big hug, it even surprised me. *Like I haven't embarrassed myself enough lately.* "I say...thank you...*muchas gracias*...thank you!" The class broke into loud cheers.

"Congratulations, Nick!" Miss Taylor said. "Even though you didn't formally try out for the part, we all agreed you'd be perfect for it. Besides, you had a very good reason for not showing up at tryouts." Strange how I felt all choked up, even though I was absolutely overjoyed.

Molly walked toward me. She had a strange grin on her face and said, "Gotcha this morning, didn't I?!" Kind of rude, but I don't think she actually meant to be mean this time. I guess, like Caroline said, it was just her attempt at being funny.

"Yeah, you got me good." It didn't even matter. I was as ecstatic as when I won the spelling bee in third grade. Besides, she really *did* get me good.

After school that day, I sprinted from the playground at top speed. Diego even had a hard time keeping up with me. I really wanted to get home fast to tell my family I got the very part I wanted. *I still can't believe they voted*

to give me that role since I didn't even try out. I better do an extra-awesome job. As soon as Mom heard the front door open, she came running. "How was your day?"

"Fantastic!!! I'm going to be Mercutio in our class play!"

My mom started clapping. "That's so exciting! How did it happen? I thought you couldn't even try out?"

"The class voted to let me have the part even though I missed tryouts. They said I was just the kind of guy who should play Mercutio. We have to wear costumes for the performance, so I'll need to get one."

"Ask Gram. I'm sure she'll make you a costume."

"I'll find pictures for her of what they wore in Italy back in the really old days."

Plink. Plunk. The keys landed in the tray, the backpack hit the wall, and Eddie bopped into the kitchen, looking for a snack. He heard the Mercutio news, and he wanted to help me learn my lines. "And if you have any kissing scenes and need some tips, I'm your guy."

"No way! Not for me. You can have those girls all to yourself." Eddie cracked up laughing. "Anyway, if anyone kisses, it will be Romeo and Juliet."

We all figured Bam would be Romeo, and I guess the teacher thought so too, 'cause he got the part. Everyone agreed Caroline was a good choice for Juliet. And Molly got her wish. She was picked for Lady Capulet. I guess most of us got the parts we'd hoped for. Some kids wanted to work behind the scenes instead of out in front. There were lots of jobs for that like painting backdrops and running lights. Obviously, Jamal would be in charge of most of that. He also had a small part as the prince. Eli got the director spot. And Sneezy was not only one of the Montagues but also—much to his terror—he was Romeo's understudy. He immediately told Bam he'd better not miss the play. The middle of May seemed light-years away, but we had a bunch of work to do before showtime.

Back at home, things were pretty calm. Katie put on a puppet show every evening. She named her puppets Romeo and Juliet. Big surprise. "Womeo, want me to sing you a song? You can't sing with me though." *Katie has a mind of her own.* "You just have to listen. 'You aw my shunshine, my only shunshine'..." The good news was tea parties seemed to be on hold for now.

Once in a while, I'd ask Mom if anyone else had said they'd try to be my kidney donor. I wanted to add more names to my secret list. "Honey, don't you worry about that. There are lots of people getting tested. One of them will be a match." Whenever I had to cross off another name, I felt empty. Even though a bunch of people were trying to be my donor—and since Mom and Dad were both off the list—my money was on Pops. I didn't tell him that. He might have felt too much pressure. *One thing's for sure...he always seems to be there when I need him the most. And boy, do I need him now.*

CHAPTER ELEVEN

"From there to here,
and here to there,
Funny things are everywhere."
—DR. SEUSS

Diego got a new bike for his birthday, and we started riding to school every day. I had my same old beat-up bike, but I didn't mind. It still worked, and...let's face it...I didn't outgrow it. At least I finally knew why. The pencil marks Dad drew on my bedroom wall to keep track of my height barely budged in two years. I guess I did gain a half inch. Better than nothing. Anyway, we got to school a lot faster than we did when we walked. Somehow, riding a bike made me feel like a free spirit. I wasn't allowed to play sports like I used to, so at least I had my wheels.

Every time I put my name on a paper at school, I added A.K.A. *Kidney Man*. All the kids in class knew that I was, in fact, the one and only Kidney Man. When I had enough time, I drew the picture Eddie and I came up with next to my name.

As the year marched on, we practiced different scenes in the play until we could do them in our sleep. Seeing the story come to life after all our hard work made us proud. We still had months to go before the performance, but we were pumped already. To top it off, I felt pretty good— no more passing out, no throwing up lately—things were looking up. I guess all that medicine did the trick.

The teacher often reminded us, "Every job in our production is important...painters, directors, stage-hands, actors...all of them." I think she wanted to make sure the actors didn't turn into braggers. Jamal recruited several kids to help with the balcony and other pieces of the set. Not me...I'm not too artsy, other than my Kidney Man pictures.

We were all surprised when Eli brought in one of his mom's lawn chairs with the words DEPUTY DIRECTOR taped to the back. He asked us to refer to him as the DD. *Sheesh.* He darted around all day with the entire script in his hand. "We'll be going off book soon, people." He even had the theater lingo down.

Molly got annoyed. "Eli, what are you talking about?"

"I mean you can't look at your script. Everyone needs to memorize their parts." He said he'd help us if we got stuck. Then he added, "You better not get stuck though. You've had plenty of time to memorize your lines." He turned into scary DD right before our eyes.

As Juliet's mother, Molly took her role a little too seriously. She ordered us around even more than usual. On the playground, she barked demands like, "Nick, do not depart so soon!" or "George! It is my will!" We got pretty good at rolling our eyes at her.

Gram came over after school one day without Pops which was strange. They're almost always together. Pops had found out a couple days before that he wasn't a match to be my donor, so I asked Gram if that's why he stayed home. "He couldn't help it, Gram...I know that." Still, he was probably disappointed, and so was I.

"He's fine, sweet pea...I just wanted to run this surprise over." She finished my costume even though we still had months to go before showtime. I never expected her to be done so fast.

"Wow! This is awesome!" The first thing I put on was a big red hat with a huge white feather in it. It looked like it belonged to a cowboy who never got dirty. The blue pants were kinda stretchy, so I could tuck them into my boots. The shirt had a ton of buttons and gigantic, fancy sleeves...it all fit perfectly. That's the sort of thing they wore way back in the Renaissance years around the 15th century.

I spotted something strange that caught my attention..."What's this for, Gram?" It kinda looked like a belt, but it had a pocket.

"That's a very important part of your costume. It will hold your prized possession!" She presented me with the coolest sword ever.

"Wow! It looks totally real!" I wasn't sure how she thought up all that creative stuff, but I was grateful. She even made me a foil-wrapped cardboard shield. The best part was the cape: it looked like Kidney Man's, except it went almost all the way down to the floor. Talk about drama! In return for her hard work, I gave Gram one of my famous squeezin' hugs.

She kept straightening my cape. "Nicholas, you'll be the best Mercutio ever!"

"Thanks, Gram...I love you so much."

I don't know if that was a crying tear in her eye, or if it was just tears caused by a really big grin. "And now, I'll start working on Benvolio's costume. You need someone to have that sword fight with!" Yep...Diego's costume was next.

Benvolio was Romeo's cousin, and Mercutio was Romeo's BFF, so Bam, D and I had a lot of scenes together. We stood on the same side of the feuding families in the story. The Montagues, Romeo's family, and the Capulets, Juliet's family, didn't like each other.

Before we even knew about the play, Jamal spent his weekends making movie clips to put online, so he took charge of videography, along with the scenery. He filmed some of the practice scenes so we could watch and learn from them. One thing we found out is that we all needed to speak louder and slower. The teacher said, "Let's get a clip of this scene with Romeo and Juliet, Jamal." She wanted us to watch so Caroline and Bam would get used to performing in front of an audience.

Caroline started…"Oh, gentle Romeo…if thou dost love me, pronounce it faithfully."

"Lady, by yonder blessed moon I vow." Just a wild guess, but I doubt Romeo and Juliet cracked up like Sam and Caroline did when they spoke those words.

Miss Taylor smiled. "That was good, you two, but Romeo and Juliet were in love. Try it again with a little more feeling and a little less giggling. Hold hands and look into each other's eyes this time. And make sure *blessed* is two syllables, Sam."

Sam reached for Caroline's hands. *I wonder how it feels to hold a girl's hand. I'm guessing it might squish like a stress ball.* They tried it again. "Oh, gentle Romeo…" But once again Bam burst out laughing.

Eli yelled, "Cut! Take three!" He was not amused.

And again…"Oh, gentle Romeo…" Bam couldn't help it. He could not control himself, and Caroline wasn't far behind. They started over five more times. By then, we were all rolling in the aisles…even the teacher and Eli.

Jamal made a decision. "We better forget about filming this scene today and try it another time."

Diego leaned over to me and whispered, "I hate to see what happens if Sam and Caroline ever *do* have to kiss on stage." D broke out into a belly laugh. "This tragedy might turn into a comedy."

Before we left to go home, Mr. Vanasco made an announcement. "Students, don't forget the Valentine's Day festival is tomorrow. Bring your families out for fun and food. The fifth grade dance will immediately follow the festival. And remember to buy your raffle tickets. We have a beautiful new bike for the lucky winner." I don't think any of the kids needed a reminder. Everyone was practically counting down the minutes till it started.

When the announcement ended, Miss Taylor added, "There's going to be a dunking booth, and I'm one of the targets this year, so bring your A-game." She winked and pretended to whisper, "I'll give you a homework pass if you miss on purpose."

Sneezy poked some fun…"Okay, Miss T. If you'll give me a homework pass, I'll make sure I throw that ball into the next booth instead of hitting the bull's eye." Ha! He wished his aim was that good.

Diego and I were in charge of setting up the cake walk booth. We had some work to do to get ready. We sketched out a plan but still had decorations to cut out and paint.

When the bell rang, I must've heard a gazillion kids say, "See you at the Valentine's Day festival tomorrow."

"If your mom says it's okay, Nick, come over to *mi casa* later and we can finish making the decorations for Saturday."

"I will, but I have to be home by eight o'clock for *you know what*. Our booth is gonna rock."

"Yeah, won't you be glad when you're done with that dialysis?"

"More than you'll ever know." *To have things back to normal would be a dream.*

D added, "And don't forget. We have to be there tomorrow by noon to set things up."

We started biking home, when George yelled, "Hey guys, stop a minute." He pulled up next to us and handed me an envelope. "This is from Caroline." He sped off before I could ask him any questions.

I opened the note and read it to myself. *What?!*

> "Hi Nick. I'm going to ask you to dance with me tomorrow. Hope that's okay."
> ♥ Caroline

My face was as red as that heart. *Why does she want to dance with me? Does she just feel sorry for me 'cause I've been sick?* I felt as nervous as I did the first time I pitched a game for my baseball team. "Diego, look at this..."

He snatched the note from my hand and quickly read it. "Whoa, Kidney Man...now who's Romeo?" He tossed it back and continued to tease me.

I raced home, locked my bike, ran into the house and up the stairs. I slid that envelope way back in the drawer next to my secret list. If Eddie knew what Caroline wrote, I'd never hear the end of it.

All of a sudden, the festival sounded even better.

CHAPTER TWELVE

"If you never did, you should.
These things are fun
and fun is good!"
—DR. SEUSS

I got up early and met Diego at school so we could help set up for the festival. Most of the booths were outside. If I still lived in Chicago instead of the desert, there'd be too much snow to have an outdoor festival in February.

Since we signed up as cake walk helpers, our booth was in the cafeteria. The decorations turned out even better than we'd hoped. It looked like a great big Valentine card. We cut out a bunch of pink cupids and red and white hearts and attached them to the wall behind our cake table. Then we taped colossal numbers from one to ten on the floor in the shape of a circle.

The cake walk was kinda like musical chairs except no one got knocked off a chair. The players walked around the circle when the music started. When it stopped— *Bingo!* The person who landed on the lucky number we pulled out of our jar won a cake.

"Check this out, Nick. I can fit this cupcake in the palm of my hand. Maybe we can fire off a few of these at the dunking booth."

"You'd have homework for the rest of your life if you did that." We laughed as I put a cupcake on my head and started speed racing around the path. It toppled over, but thankfully, I caught it before it splattered.

"No, wait...this is better." Diego grabbed one of the regular-size cakes and put that on his head. "These bigger ones will stay on longer. Let's have a little race before we get any customers." We probably should've known better after our hospital fiasco, but it never even entered our minds.

Eli walked up just as we discussed our plan to see which of us could get to the drinking fountain first. "Dude, we have to pick two cakes about the same size to keep it fair. Deal?"

"Deal."

Eli chimed in, "Uh, guys...bad idea. Those cakes are too unstable to balance on your heads. Remember...what goes up, must come down. If you make a quick turn, you'll mess up your center of gravity and your cake will hit the ground."

Gravity-smavity. We weren't worried. We both

oozed with confidence—a little too much may-be—'cause as soon as Eli blew the start whistle and we took off walking, both our cakes fell off our heads and splattered all over the place.

Eli shook his head in disgust. "I told you."

Diego mumbled, "¡Oh, Dios Mío! Guess we should've listened."

I added, "OMG is right."

"I heard that a guy balanced a milk bottle on his head and walked for eighty miles. That was a record. Guess you guys won't be smashing any records today...just cakes." Eli laughed at his own joke. I don't think he felt sorry for us at all. One thing's for sure...we had a big gooey, sprinkly, chocolatey mess to clean up.

"Oh no," Diego complained, "the cake got all over my shirt!"

"Forget about your shirt! Look at the floor. We better get rid of the evidence before our parents see it."

"There's the custodian's broom and mop," Diego said. "I don't think he'll mind if we borrow them."

"Dang! Too late. Our moms are headed this way." The closer they got, the faster they walked.

Diego's mom let out a tiny shriek as she slid on a little patch of icing. I grabbed for her hand to keep her from falling. "What on Earth happened here?" She looked at her son. "Diego! You have a lot of explaining to do! What do you have to say for yourself?"

Realizing I was next, I glanced over at my mom. "And Nick, do you understand that volunteers put time and effort into baking those cakes you just destroyed?"

"Well…" I stammered. "I'm so sorry. It was a stupid idea. I swear I'll never do anything like that again."

Diego chimed in, attempting to save me. "It wasn't our best moment. We'll clean up every single drop. Sorry you slipped, Mom. Are you okay?"

"Oh, Diego…I'm fine, but you two better get rid of this mess fast."

Our moms walked away together, no doubt planning our punishment for later. "That's what you call bad timing, D."

We cleaned up, then worked the booth like pros. As soon as our hour was up, some of the adults took over. Diego exclaimed, "Let's get this party started!"

"First, we need to wash this cake off our shirts," I said.

"Okay, but then…straight to the dunking tank."

"Good idea. Miss Taylor should be in there by now."

There was a big line, but it moved quickly. A sign hanging near the dunk tank read: *Want to send your teacher for a plunge? One ticket gets you a baseball to throw at the bull's eye.*

"There's Miss T up on the perch, Nick. Somebody must've nailed that target." She was dripping wet and shivering.

Diego was up first. He yelled, "Get ready to hold your breath, Miss Taylor!" She made a gesture like she was begging him to miss. He did a very long windup, then took his best shot. Lucky for her, he was off by a mile…and not on purpose either.

"NEXT." I gave the guy my ticket, and he tossed me a ball. Just then, Caroline and some other girls walked up beside us.

Here come those butterflies again. I managed to blurt out, "Hey, Caroline. How's it going?"

"Good. Looks like you're up next." She smiled at me.

"Well, I think I'll say, 'Ladies first.'" I stepped aside and handed her the ball I'd paid for. To tell the truth, I just didn't want to embarrass myself in front of her if I had a bad throw.

"Are you sure? It's your turn."

"No, please...go ahead. My treat." *Oh, man...I sound like my father.*

She fired at the target and hit it smack in the middle of the bull's eye. Down went Miss Taylor into the cold water. Caroline put her hands over her face like she was embarrassed her secret was out. Who knew she had an arm like a big league pitcher!

Everyone cheered, but it quickly died down as our drenched teacher popped out of the water. Someone threw her a towel as she yelled, "Caroline! Again?" *Geez...She must've gotten her twice!* Miss T laughed...a good sport, as usual. She was probably relieved it was the end of her shift.

The star pitcher glanced my way. "Wow! That was amazing, Caroline!" I gave her a high-five and so did all her friends. "See you later at the dance."

"Can't wait," Caroline said, "and thanks for the ball." I smiled so hard my cheeks hurt, and with that, the girls went in the other direction. I didn't even bother trying to hit the target after that. Instead, Diego and I headed off to the football booth.

"Bro, you were as smooth as a baby's bottom back there."

"Actually, I was ready to jump out of my skin, but then I thought, that's crazy. Caroline and I have been friends since kindergarten. She might be a girl, but she's also a friend."

"That's a fact. Very mature of you, Nick. Let's see which booth we can tackle next."

We had as much luck tossing footballs through hanging car tires as we did throwing baseballs. We walked around and looked at all the other games. We picked up a few trinkets here and there. I think every kid in the school was at that festival.

The loud speaker crackled to life. The principal was ready to announce the winner of the raffle. The bike they were giving away was a brand new BMX racing bike. I never won anything, but I took some of the money I earned mowing the lawn and bought a few tickets anyway. I wanted to hear the results, so D and I moved closer to the action.

Mr. Vanasco really built up the excitement. "Is everybody ready?!..." We all started screaming. "I can't hear you!" We screamed louder. He waved the winning ticket in the air for a very long few seconds, then announced..."The lucky winner of this beautiful white bicycle is...Katie Cicero."

"What?!! My little sister won?"

Diego added, "Wow! I can't believe it!"

"Let's head over there, D. I guess my dad bought Katie a ticket. Can't believe that bike is hers!"

We could see Katie jumping up and down, and we heard her yelling, "I won! I won!" My parents were up by the microphone talking to Mr. V and helping my sister collect her prize. As I walked toward them, Katie made a beeline straight for me. Clearly, she had spent some time at the face painting booth. Bright purple and blue, neon-colored flowers decorated her eyes, and glittery yellow stars ran down the sides of her face. She sure was sparkly...and very excited.

I hugged her. "Congratulations, Katie! You'll have to put that new bike away until you grow taller though."

"I want you to have my bwan new bike." My sister reached for my hand like she was handing me the keys to her car.

"You don't have to do that. Maybe we could trade it for one that's just your size." *I mean, yeah, I'd love that bike, but I don't want to take it from her.*

"No, Nic-o-wis. It will make you feel bett-aw."

I tried to read my dad's face to see if it was true. "Dad, really?"

Mom said, "She wants to do this. Just say thanks to your generous little sister." She squeezed us both at the same time.

I couldn't believe I had a brand new bike. "Thank you, thank you, thank you, thank you, Katie!" I said.

"You're the best sister in the history of the world!" Katie giggled as Dad grabbed her and threw her up in the air.

Just when I thought things were as good as they could possibly get, Mr. Vanasco came back on the loud-speaker and said, "Fifth-grade students and their chaperones may head to the gym for our annual dance." Yes! The wait was finally over.

CHAPTER THIRTEEN

"...Just never forget
to be dexterous and deft
And never mix up your right foot
with your left."
—DR. SEUSS

D and I were some of the first kids in the dance hall...A.K.A. our school's gym. It sure didn't look like the place where we played basketball. The Student Council had decorated, and they went all out. Jamal made a sign for the door that read, "Welcome, Fifth Graders!" He drew musical notes all over it. If I would've created that sign, it would look like one of Katie's art projects. But not Jamal...his quarter notes were as bright as the colors in my kaleidoscope.

We walked through a tall archway made of pink

and white balloons. There were 3-D cupids and paper hearts of different sizes all over the walls. The hearts reminded me of those little candy ones. They had sayings like *Be mine* and *Crazy* 4U printed on them. Silvery, lighted trees decorated with dangling red bulbs brightened all four corners of the room.

It didn't take long for the gym to fill up with lots of kids and loud music. In the beginning, we just stood around. It was our first dance, and we were all clueless. We leaned awkwardly against the walls. It felt a little weird, but then the cousins got things fired up. As soon as they hit the dance floor and busted a move, a bunch of kids joined them, including D and me.

Sneezy said, "This is awesome!" He spun around two times on the floor. I didn't know he even had moves like that. Molly waved her arms all over the place. Eli played the air guitar. Bam and Jamal didn't leave the wall. They weren't really into dancing. The music pounded, and the DJ played all the songs we liked. We could barely hear each other speak. I decided to go find Gram and Pops. They were chaperones, and I wanted to see if they were wearing earplugs yet.

"How are you feeling, Nicholas?" Grandma yelled over the music. I think that was the first time I ever heard her say my actual name. She must've known I'd be embarrassed if she called me sweet pea in front of everyone.

"I feel great, Gram."

Pops walked over, and we did our special handshake.

"Do you want me to go out on that floor and show you kids how it's done?"

I smiled. "Maybe in a little while."

"Take it easy, Joe. You don't want to make that cough of yours any worse. In our day, Nick, your grandfather danced better than anyone around. He even won a contest when he was younger." Grandma winked at him. "That's why I married you, Joe." She always kidded him about that.

My grandmother seemed concerned about me. "You're all sweaty. Go grab yourself a drink." She pointed to the snack bar. "Looks like your friends are over there getting lemonade. They have some ice cold water. A little cup of it would probably hit the spot after all that dancing."

I looked over and saw Caroline and her posse of girls. *Am I brave enough to walk over to their group?* There was a good chance my hands would shake when I held the drink. *Oh no...She's heading this way.*

"Hey, Nick. Save a dance for me later?"

"Of course. Let's wait for a good song to come on though..." *Really? That's all I got here? Too bad Grandma had to hear my dumb answer.*

"Sounds good. I'll come and find you again."

Caroline and her crew got excited when they heard...*It's Electric!* They ran out to get in the dance line. I'd learned how to do "The Electric Slide" at my cousin's wedding, but I decided to sit this one out. Naturally, Diego ended up in the middle of the posse, and he loved every minute of it.

The next song came on, and Pops couldn't wait any longer. I noticed he was in an extra-good mood. He cruised onto the floor, inserted himself right in the middle of everyone...and taught them his favorite new dance, "The Wobble." I felt that beat rising up in me and before I could even think about it, I headed back out there too.

Pretty soon, a big circle formed. The Matts jumped in the middle, spinning and doing flips. They pointed at Diego, and he leaped right in. He was probably glad he brought his fedora with him. That added an extra cool factor.

Pops leaned over to me wearing a huge smile on his face. I thought he was going to tell me to get in there next. Instead he said, "I was going to wait until tomorrow to tell you this...but I'm about to burst and can't hold it in for another second!"

"What's going on?" He had me excited, and I didn't even know why.

"You know I didn't think I could give you a kidney, right?"

"Yeah..."

I strained my ears to hear him, but it was tough because the kids started yelling, "Kid-ney Man!" They wanted me to get in the circle.

My grandfather shouted over them. "Well, several of us were put on a *pairing* list. I was approved to donate one of my kidneys to a needy older person so you could get a kidney from someone younger who's a perfect match."

"What?! So we're swapping kidneys with someone? Do they allow that kind of thing?"

"Yes! Even though my kidney won't work for you, it will work for someone else." He hugged me extra hard. We both had tears in our eyes. *Who cares if I can't trade lunches at school? We're trading kidneys!*

"Now go have fun." Pops started coughing again, and he was out of breath.

"Too much dancing, Grandpa?"

"Guess this old man got carried away." He laughed. "I'm going to leave it to you young people for a while."

Before he left, I grabbed him again and said, "I *knew* it would be you." I could tell that meant a lot to him. He put his palm on his heart.

The kids' volume went up about ten notches. "Kid-ney Man! Kid-ney Man!"

I jumped into the center of the circle and laid it all out on the dance floor. I did moves I didn't even know I had. Maybe it was my imagination, but it seemed like everyone was as overjoyed as I was at that moment, even though they didn't know my news yet—they just wanted me to get in the middle of the dance circle.

The song changed, and Caroline walked my way. It was now or never.

"Will this song work?" She gave me a little grin.

I tried to keep my voice calm and said, "It's perfect." There was no getting around the fact that it was a slow song, and I had a serious case of drippy palms. She put both her hands on my shoulders. I wasn't sure what to do with mine, so I just put them on her waist. I didn't really touch her—just her clothes—so there's no way she knew about the sweaty palms.

We danced awkwardly and chatted like the old friends we were. "This night has been more fun than I even thought it would be, Nick. I was worried that no one would dance, but instead *everyone* is dancing. "

"Yeah," I said. "The cousins got us all going."

"Remember when we had square dancing in second grade PE class? I loved that pink cowgirl hat I got to wear."

"Oh man! How could I forget?! None of us wanted to do-si-do, but it was kind of like our first dance in a way."

The song ended, and so did the dance. Dancing with Caroline was the icing on the cake, which was much better than having the icing all over the floor.

On the way home from the dance, Pops hummed all the tunes, and Gram sang along with him. When we reached my house, I said, "You're coming in to tell my family about the kidney pairing, aren't you?"

Pops' eyes twinkled. "Sure."

We walked into the living room where my parents were watching the news. Dad always had the same channel on TV. He's worse than I am with the Cartoon Network.

"From that smile I see on your face, honey, the dance must've been a success."

"It was the best, Mom! But we have some *major* news."

"What's going on? Did something happen?"

"It sure did, but it had nothing to do with dancing. Pops figured out a way to get me a kidney!"

A big smile filled Mom's face. "He told you?" She looked over at her father.

"Wait...you mean I was the last to know?" *Come on, people, it's my body part.*

"Dad, I thought you were going to surprise him with that news tomorrow at dinner?"

"It just popped out of my mouth, Maur. The moment seemed right."

Grandma chuckled. "In all the years I've known him, sweet pea, your grandfather's never been able to keep a secret."

Before I climbed into bed, I dug the list out of the back of my drawer. I erased the line I'd drawn through Pops' name. It was definitely the best day of my life.

CHAPTER FOURTEEN

"I've heard there are troubles
of more than one kind.
Some come from ahead,
some come from behind."

—DR. SEUSS

Grandpa came over before school on Monday to hang out with Katie so Mom could run errands. I didn't feel like going to school that day. Maybe because we had such an incredible weekend, and I hated to see it end. I was worn out from all the excitement. I just wanted to stay home.

"Nick, let's take care of your medicine before it gets too late." Mom always tried to say that in a cheery way, but I wasn't up for it today. She probably wasn't either.

Was I sick of being sick? I just wanted it all to be

over. Whoever heard of needing shots to grow any-way? I thought kids grew on their own. Then there's the bazillion pills...ugh. How much can one kid stand?!

"Hey, Mom...maybe I can skip these pills and shots since I'll be getting a kidney soon?"

"I'm sorry...that's not possible. Now, let's get it over with quickly. You can't be late for school."

"Give me a minute..." I just wanted to complain to Grandpa. He always gave me the sympathy I needed.

I walked onto the screened in porch where I saw Pops lying in the hammock. *That's where I'd like to be all day today.* I began my rant. "I'm sick and tired of taking all this medicine." He looked up at me, but he didn't get up.

"You've been a real trooper through all of this, buddy. You'll handle it." He didn't seem to have much energy either. He wasn't killing any flies, which was what he normally did when he was on the porch. In fact, he looked a little pale to me. I decided to stop grumbling and leave him alone. I went back inside and took my shots without another peep.

"Why the change of heart?" Mom seemed surprised I'd stopped complaining.

I thought about how my grandfather looked. "Is Pops okay? Usually he has way more energy."

"As far as I know, he's fine, but I'll check on him after you leave. He probably danced one too many times. He needs to take it easy to get rid of his cough, so he's in good shape to donate his kidney for the pairing."

"Okay, well I'm outta here. Love you, Mom." I was anxious to jump on my brand new bike. Thanks to Katie.

"Love you, too, Nicholas. Have a gr-r-r-eat day!" The door slammed behind me just as Diego pulled into the driveway.

"Hop on those new wheels and let's hit the road. Bet I can beat you to school!" Diego took off while I was still putting on my bike helmet.

"Cheater!..." With my new bike, I caught up to him in no time. I couldn't wait to use that shiny, silver combination lock Pops gave me.

At school, we all buzzed about the dance. In fact, that's all we talked about all morning. I was kind of proud of myself because I didn't even get clammy palms this time when I saw Caroline. Probably because she and her friends had called me on the phone Sunday. We talked and joked around. I'm not sure who mentioned it first, but we decided to keep this thing in the friend zone. I mean, we're only fifth graders. Anyway, neither one of us wanted to get all mushy about it.

When the last bell rang, I headed for the bike rack. When I pulled into our driveway, I was surprised to see Dad's car there...it was pretty early for him to be home from work. I ran in the house to investigate. Velcro met me at the door. I could always depend on him to miss me. Dad was sitting at the kitchen table, but Mom was nowhere in sight. Katie was playing with her dolls in the family room. The look on Dad's face told me something was off.

"What are you doing home already?" I went over and gave him a half hug.

"Can't I be home in the middle of the day?" He smiled like he was trying to kid around, but he couldn't pull it off.

"Where's Mom? And Pops? I thought he was watching Katie today? I wanted to tell him my combination lock worked great."

"Nick, your mom said when you left this morning, you didn't think your grandfather looked too good." *Why am I feeling nervous all of a sudden?* "And, unfortunately, you were right."

"What happened to him? Where is he?" My mind raced.

"Grandpa thought he had a cold, but right after you left for school this morning, he started coughing up blood. He's in the hospital. Mom's there with him and so is Grandma. When Eddie gets home, I'm going to head over there too." *No! This can't be happening. First my stinkin' kidneys...and now this?*

"How sick is he?" *I mean, is he dying or what?*

"I'm afraid he's in rough shape, son. They did a chest X-ray and found something suspicious. It could be blood in his lungs. We don't know much more than that yet, but the doctors are running tests to see what their next step will be."

"I want to see him." I needed to tell him not to worry about giving me his kidney.

"He's in a special unit, so we'll have to ask the doctors. Let's see how he feels later today. Maybe Eddie can drive you to the hospital after Mrs. Kelly picks up Katie for ballet class."

I had to see my grandfather, and I was glad Dad seemed to understand that.

When Eddie got home from school, Dad left. I was in my bedroom and Katie walked in. "Nic-o-wis, I need a snack."

"Get a snack then, Katie. I'm not your waiter."

She looked at me and said, "Why aw you mad?"

"Grandpa is super sick right now. I'm just worried about him."

"Should we dwaw him a picha?"

"Yeah, it couldn't hurt. What do you want for a snack?" I felt bad that I'd snapped at my little sister. I walked out to the kitchen with her. She decided to eat it on the couch in front of the TV. That was fine with me.

"Here are your colors and art paper, if you want to make Grandpa a picture."

"Thanks. He's gonna wuv it."

Eddie sat there with his headphones on. *Some babysitter he is.* I grabbed his headphones and yelled, "You might want to pay attention to our four-year-old sister. She could burn the house down and you wouldn't even know it."

"Oh, I'd smell that for sure…" He thinks everything's a big joke.

I went back to my room. I got out my secret list and

unfolded it. I saw Pops' name on there. I had to cross it off again. The last line on my list was the only one that wasn't crossed out...get a kidney from a deceased donor. It felt like someone punched me in the gut and knocked the wind out of me. *There's no one left! I may never get a kidney now.* All I could think of was what Eli said. "Did you know that thirteen people die each day waiting for kidney transplants?" The professor wasn't too great at knowing when to keep his thoughts to himself. His words played over and over in my head.

I also couldn't get the thought of Pops lying in a hospital bed out of my head. Life was closing in on me. I ripped my list up into as many pieces as I could and threw it on the floor. I kicked the trash can, and it smashed into the wall. I knocked the trophies I got for a spelling bee and flag football onto the floor. Then I threw myself onto the bed. I sobbed into my pillow. I couldn't bear it if something happened to my grandfather. My tears wouldn't stop flowing.

Katie must've heard the crash. She was standing at my door. "Nic-o-wis, are you sad?"

"Leave me alone, Katie. I don't feel good." She left and shut the door behind her. The doorbell rang. She must've come in to say goodbye before Mrs. Kelly picked her up for dance class. I felt like a jerky big brother again.

The pain of Grandpa's sickness was way worse than the pain from any shots I had to take. It came from deep inside. My pillow was soaked with tears. I cried the way a baby does...almost wailing, but I couldn't seem to stop. After a few minutes, I heard a knock on the door. I looked up, and Eddie was standing there. Katie must've told him I didn't feel good.

"Get lost, Eddie." I didn't need him making fun of me on top of everything else.

He came over and sat on the edge of my bed. He put his hand on my back. I tried to catch my breath, then I looked up at him, wondering what he was doing. He picked me up off the bed and hugged me. "I'm sad, too, Nick." I sobbed in his arms. Eddie cried right along with me. "Grandpa's going to be okay. We just have to have faith in the doctors." This was a different Eddie. *What have you done with my brother?*

I agreed with him. "That's all we got at this point."

Eddie stood up and tossed me a couple tissues. "Get cleaned up, Kidney Man. Let's go to the hospital."

CHAPTER FIFTEEN

"Kid, you'll move mountains!
Today is your day!
Your mountain is waiting.
So...get on your way."
—DR. SEUSS

Eddie drove us to the hospital. It seemed strange going through those doors as a visitor instead of a patient. A volunteer brought us to the Intensive Care Unit. In the elevator on the way up to the fourth floor, I tried to picture Pops in a hospital bed, but I just couldn't do it. My mind raced...please be okay...please be okay...as if the more I thought it, the better he would be. He was always full of energy, so I had no idea how he'd look or how I'd feel when I saw him. I only knew that I wanted to see him.

We met Dad in the waiting room, and he walked Eddie back first to see Grandpa. I alternated between playing games on my phone and watching the doctors and nurses pass by the doorway. They were always in a big hurry to get somewhere. I thought I might see someone I knew, but I was on another floor when I was a patient. Different faces...same sounds. The lady on the loudspeaker still paged someone every other minute. The elevators chimed each time the door opened. One thing's for sure: I felt more stressed sitting in the waiting room than I did being the one in bed.

I looked up from my game and was surprised to see my social worker walk in. "Hi, Christina. What are you doing at the hospital?"

"I have an office upstairs. I ran into your mom a while ago. She said I'd find you in this waiting area, so I thought I'd stop by to see how you're holding up."

"I've been better. Do you think it's my fault my grandfather got so sick? I asked him to chaperone the dance, but maybe that was too much."

"Yes, your grandfather's in the hospital, but it had nothing to do with you needing a kidney." I could tell Christina was a little worried about me. "I brought you a gift." She reached into her pocket. "This is something you can wear on your wrist to help you remember what we always talk about."

She handed me a red, rubber bracelet. It said *The Power of Yet*. I knew exactly what that meant. "Thank you." I looked up through my tears and gave her half a smile. "I don't have a new kidney YET...but I will."

"Exactly." It struck me then that anything is possible...we just have to be patient.

Right then, my brother came through the waiting room door. "Okay, Nick...your turn."

Oh geez. I started feeling nervous, like I'd never spoken to my grandfather before. "What am I gonna' say?"

Eddie came over and sat in the chair next to me. "He'll just be happy to see your face." Christina nodded in agreement.

I tried to coax myself into a better frame of mind as I walked down the long hall to the intensive care unit. I squeezed that red bracelet with all my might. *Pops isn't better YET, but he will be with time.* I passed the nurses' station. I knew that's what they called it from when I was a patient. This floor was a little different than the one I'd been on. The nurses were in the middle and there were about eight rooms around their station. Funny how the intensive care unit is nicknamed ICU, and the nurses really *can* C U when you're a patient in there.

My mother stood outside Grandpa's room, waiting for me. She looked worn out. "He's anxious to see you, Nick."

"Mom, maybe this wasn't such a good idea. I don't think I can go in there."

She grabbed my cheeks and said, "Yes you can, honey." She always told me I had courage bubbling up inside me, waiting to get out. *Right now I think those bubbles are as flat as yesterday's pancakes.*

Grandma sat in the corner of the room, gazing out the window. She jumped up when I walked in, then reached for my hands and kissed my forehead. "He just dozed off for a second, sweet pea. Go stand closer so he'll see you when he wakes up."

I got that pain in the back of my throat that happens when you're trying to hold back tears. I didn't want him to see me cry. I'm pretty sure people did the same thing when I was the one in the bed because, come to think of it, I didn't see waterworks from anyone.

I walked over, stared down at his face, and noticed how peaceful he looked sleeping. I didn't want to wake him—maybe I even wanted to sneak out before I actually had to talk to him. I reached down and lightly put my fist on his hand—the beginning of our special hand-shake. He opened his eyes and smiled.

"Hi, Pops." I gave his fingers a little squeeze. His hands were cold. I whispered, "This is a pretty extreme way to get people to wait on you." He always liked a good joke, even if it wasn't very funny.

"Yeah…" The side of his mouth turned up just a lit-tle to show the start of a smile. "Nick…I'm so sorry…I wanted to give you my kidney more than anything, but now I don't know—"

I didn't let him finish that sentence. "Yeah, well I *do* know. If it was possible, you'd do anything for me, and I'd do anything for you." His misty eyes looked even bluer against his tanned, wrinkled face. "So, just get yourself back in shape. Don't worry about me 'cause the Kidney Man has a kidney plan." I had no clue what the plan was YET.

My determination was clear, and he chuckled. "Go get 'em, partner..."

Before I left the room, I blew Grandma a kiss.

Mom stood outside the door, waiting. "Are you okay?"

"You know something?" I said with about as much certainty as I'd ever had. "You might be right about that courage bubbling up inside me." Mom smiled. I'd seen so many sick people in the hospital bravely facing their challenges; I figured it was time I did that, too.

She said, "Say some prayers, Nick." I walked down the hall, touching my bracelet and looking for Eddie. I would definitely say prayers for Grandpa, but I was also going to figure out, once and for all, how to get myself a kidney. Enough already.

CHAPTER SIXTEEN

> "Now my troubles are going to
> have troubles with me!"
> —DR. SEUSS

On the drive back home, Eddie blasted his music, so I didn't need to talk much. That was fine with me 'cause my mind was like a ping pong ball. It bounced back and forth from Pops lying in that hospital bed to me finding a kidney. If I could come up with a plan, we'd all have one less thing to worry about. I got tired of waiting around for something to happen. Too bad I couldn't just wave some sort of magic wand. I needed a brainstorm.

That night, Dad came into my bedroom to hook up the

cycler. I didn't notice him talking to me, so he waved his hand in front of my face to break the trance. "Hey, Nick, where are you?"

"Sorry, Dad, I was just thinking."

"Must be some pretty deep thoughts."

"Yep, you could say that." Figuring out how to get a kidney wouldn't be easy for any kid.

"Good news...Grandma just called to say that your grandfather is going to be okay. The doctors put a tube down his throat to check things out. They discovered inflammation in his blood vessels. He'll have to take medication for a long time, but he'll be on the road to recovery very soon!"

"What a relief!" I didn't understand most of what he said. What I did hear was that Pops would be okay.

"It's been a long day. Try to get some rest. Maybe we can all sleep peacefully tonight." Dad left the room and Velcro took his position next to my bed. He let out one of his biggest yawns yet. I guess he'd had a tough day too 'cause the snoring started the minute his head hit that dog bed.

I finally managed to nod off. I woke up in the middle of the night though...and it wasn't because the alarm on my cycler blared. I had a dream that seemed so real it jolted me out of a deep sleep. I mean, I really thought it was happening.

I was carrying a big sign stuck to a pole—kind of like the one Eddie drew when he said, "Will work for kidney." It looked like the banners the protesters on the news hold when they march for special causes. This time, the sign said, "Save the Kidney Man!" In my dream, I paraded all over town, and a bunch of people trailed after me yelling, "Kid-Ney Man! Kid-Ney Man!" It's weird how your mind can create a place you've never seen and a bunch of people with no faces.

I think that dream was some kind of omen. Right out loud, I said, "That's it! I'll launch a campaign…*with a little help from my friends*, as the song goes." Dad plays the Beatles a lot. "We'll tell everyone, everywhere that I need a kidney!" Velcro opened one eye and looked at me when he heard my voice. The only sounds were his whimper and the humming of my cycler.

He grumbled, then licked his lips and yawned. I took that as "Yeah, good idea, kid."

I decided I'd talk about my plan the next day at school. It was just the kinda thing the kids would get fired up about.

My head hit the pillow again. I think I still had a big grin on my face when I zonked out. Clearly, some of my best brainstorms come to me while I'm snoozing.

CHAPTER SEVENTEEN

"So open your mouth, lad!
For every voice counts!"
—DR. SEUSS

We talked about Pops' good news at breakfast the next morning. We were so relieved that, even though he'd probably be in the hospital a little longer, he was going to be okay.

Everyone rushed to leave on time. Mom had to drop Katie off at Mrs. Kelly's house before she headed to the hospital. Dad sprinted out the door to work. Eddie was long gone. And I didn't even have time to tell them about my dream.

I noticed the newspaper on the table as I was eating my eggs. It was open to the page called *Letters to the Editor* where people write about different topics that rile them or make them super happy. Dad reads one to Mom every morning. The editor of the paper responds sometimes. But other times, there's no response. They just print what the person had to say. *Hmm...what if—*

Diego rang the doorbell, and I yelled, "C'mon in." I grabbed the scissors and furiously started cutting.

"Dude...what are you doing? What's the holdup?"

"I'll tell you later. It's something very big, but you're just gonna have to wait."

We biked to school in record time, and I talked at record speed. I did tell him all about Pops, and he sure was happy to hear that good news. I didn't say a word about my new plan though. I wanted him to hear it when everyone else did.

As the clock struck two, Miss Taylor started our class meeting. "The first and only item on our agenda this afternoon is from Mr. Cicero. Go for it, Nick...What do you want to share?"

"Okay." I cleared my throat. "You guys know how I've been waiting to get a kidney, right?" The kids all stared at me and kind of shook their heads and mumbled, "Yes."

The teacher chimed in. "We're very aware of your situation, Nick, and I'm sure every single one of us hopes you get a kidney soon."

"Well, I was hoping you might feel that way. You guys have been on my side through all of this." The kids did their silent thumbs-up cheer. "It might sound weird, but I had a dream last night that woke me up from a deep sleep." I heard a few chuckles. "Seriously, I'm not even making this stuff up. So, I was carrying one of those signs like they do at protests. It said *Save the Kidney Man.* I was parading up and down streets holding it high in the air. Tons of people were walking behind me yelling, 'Kid-ney Man! Kid-ney Man!' They were trying to help me."

Bam interrupted, "Maybe that was us."

"I couldn't see their faces, Sam, but I thought the same thing. When I woke up, what I needed to do was clear to me. But only if you guys are willing to help."

Diego couldn't keep quiet anymore. He raised his hand, and the teacher handed him the microphone. "I think I speak for everyone, *amigo*, when I say we'll do whatever we can to help you get a kidney." All the kids held their thumbs up again and pumped them like crazy.

"I knew I could count on you!" I said, as I looked around the circle at Miss Taylor. "May I use the document camera?"

"Go for it, Nick."

I placed the letter that I cut out of the newspaper under the camera. Eli hopped up to help me adjust it just right.

"Members of the class, please lend me your ear…" I thought I'd throw in some Shakespeare-type talk to get them interested. "Some of you might've heard of letters to the editor."

The teacher jumped in to clarify. "Has anyone ever read one of them in our local newspaper?"

Caroline answered, "My neighbor wrote a letter to the editor because he was upset about a tax he had to pay."

"Exactly right, Caroline."

Jamal took the microphone and said, "It reminds me of *The Rant* they have on the news. My dad loves that. People rant about issues that make them mad. I guess they probably tell positive stuff, too—although I've never heard much of that."

"Yes, very similar, Jamal. Okay, so Nick..." The teacher wanted to move this along before the bell rang. "Tell us, fine sir. What exactly do you have in mind?"

"I want to put together a *Save the Kidney Man* campaign to spread the word about organ donation. We can start by writing letters like this one to the editor. We can tell the readers there are thousands of people out there waiting for organ donations, myself included. We'll ask them to consider being donors. We could all write letters, and maybe we'd get lucky, and they'd publish one of them."

"Well, we won't know until we try." I knew Miss Taylor would approve. "And you know I'm all about writing projects," she joked.

The microphone was passed to Eli. "I just read last night there are over a hundred thousand people on the national transplant waiting list, but less than half of the population has signed up as donors." Our faces dropped. "People need to realize they're missing an opportunity to save lives." *Well said, Eli.*

I fell into teacher mode. "Let's include facts about kidney disease in our letters. We'll flood the editor's mailbox!"

Jamal added, "We should figure out exactly what we want to say so our message is strong." *And that's why he gets all A's.*

"I know what *I'm* going to write," Sneezy got all serious for a minute. "I'll tell the readers that my dad would still be alive if he could've gotten a heart transplant." The class got completely silent.

"George, that's all the more reason to put everything we've got into this campaign," Miss Taylor's eyes welled up when she said that.

Molly chimed in with something that surprised me. "You guys have seen my dad on *Channel 8 News*, right?" *Seen him? You brag about him ten times a day.* "I could ask him to do a story on this. He likes what he calls *human interest pieces.*"

"Molly, that would be fantastic!" For once, she was actually being helpful. "Miss Taylor, what do you think?"

"Nick, I love it. The bell's about to ring, but I'll allot some time in our day tomorrow to get this plan in motion. Put those brains of yours into high gear, everyone. Let's come up with our very best ideas."

"Thanks, guys," I said. "You're the best." I saw a few kids go over to Sneezy and give him a pat on the shoulder. My friends were already buzzing with ideas.

The bell rang and we all rushed to get our backpacks ready to go home. "Kidney Man, we got this." I looked up and saw George. "There's no way I'm going to let this happen again to anybody I know." *I sure hope he's right.*

CHAPTER EIGHTEEN

"Just tell yourself, Duckie,
you're really quite lucky."
—DR. SEUSS

I rode my bicycle up our driveway as fast as I could. I always go into the house through the garage, and I was glad to see Mom's car in there. She was on the porch, coloring with Katie.

"Mom, if you're not at the hospital, Pops must be feeling pretty good today?" I almost hated to ask because I couldn't bear it if anything had changed.

"Gwampa is aw betta today." Katie must've been wondering who would wear that crown if Pops didn't get home soon.

"Your sister's right, Nick. He looked great this morning, and the doctors believe he's recuperating nicely.

I let out a little *woo-hoo*. Katie joined in with me.

"You won't believe what happened at school today!"

"Oh yeah?"

"I had a dream last night…"

Mom looked at me, confused—or *corn-fused*, as she likes to say.

"I asked the class if they would help me start a *Save the Kidney Man* campaign. We already came up with a ton of great ideas." I babbled on, filling Mom in on the dream, the kids' suggestions for helping me get a new kidney, and the letters we were all writing to the editor. "Isn't it great?"

"Isn't what great?" I didn't hear Eddie come in, but he was already chowing down on a bag of microwave popcorn. Man, that looked good, but of course, *his* popcorn was smothered in cheese and salt.

"Eddie, eat that in the kitchen." Mom gave him a *You know better than that, mister* kind of look. They try to keep tempting food like that out of my view. I can eat popcorn, but I can't have the salty toppings. "Your brother just told me his ideas on how he can persuade people to be organ donors and try to get a kidney." Mom nodded at Eddie, egging him on to speak positively to me. Instead, she kept talking…"Honey, as we've all learned, there's a lot that goes into finding a kidney donor. You can't just *ask* for one." It was obvious she didn't want me to get my hopes up. *Too late.*

"Mom, remember, you always say that having a good thought is free, and it sure does make me feel better."

Her face lit up like something just dawned on her. She wrote with crayon on Katie's picture: "GO FOR IT, KIDNEY MAN!" I let her slide this time on calling me by my nickname, since she didn't actually say it out loud. That was reserved for friends.

"Thanks, Mom. This is going to be really something...you'll see."

"Little bro, I just might have a few ideas up my sleeve to help you spread the word."

"Really?" I didn't expect Eddie to help. *It's like he flips from mean older brother to lifelong best friend in the blink of an eye.* "Like what?"

"Well, I just saw a video where a dude asked people to donate to a fund for his niece who was in a bad accident. Her medical costs were piling up. We could make a video of you telling people how important organ donation is and how you could use a kidney yourself, if anyone has a spare. I mean...why not, right?" Eddie was always on the computer, and he knew all about posting videos.

"You thought of that idea fast, Ed!" *There ya go. Fast Eddie.* He needed a nickname. "I'll have to figure out what to say on the video though."

"I know what you can say, Nicowis...Woses aw wed. Vie-wits aw bwue. I need a kidney...fwom you and you." Katie pointed at Eddie and me when she said, "You and you."

"Katie...that was *fantástico!*" You could tell my brother was taking a Spanish class at school...and he was proud of our little sister. "Maybe you'll be a famous poet like Shel Silverstein someday." He poked her belly to make her giggle. Works every time.

"Special delivery for the best sister in the entire world…" I held a paper over her head as she jumped up to reach it. I guess I'm carrying on some of Eddie's torture rituals.

"Give it to me." I let it drift down so it landed in her hands. "Foe me?"

"Yep, just for you. I wanted to make sure you knew how much I LOVE my new bike!" She stared at the picture I drew for her. Mom looked over her shoulder and read it out loud.

"Wow," Mom said. "Look at you getting a thank you card for being so generous to your brother. We're proud of you." Katie grinned from ear to ear.

My brother grabbed his laptop off the table. He played around on it while I helped my sister finish coloring her picture. Then Eddie said, "Look at this…a social media storm is key." I glanced at the screen and saw that he already made me my very own *Save the Kidney Man* page. "We can post your video here. We'll put a picture of your *Kidney Man* character right at the top. You'll be legendary in no time."

"I hope you're right."

"Come on. You should know by now that I'm always right." Even fast Eddie laughed at that one.

⚡

The next day in class, the kids were bursting with ideas for our campaign, so we worked on it first thing. Caroline said, "My sister is on the high school basketball team. She and her teammates decided to have a car wash and donate the proceeds to the Kidney Foundation in your name, Nick. They want to raise awareness about CKD. The top shooter on her team has it."

"She does?" *Some kids with this disease must still be able to play sports.* "A car wash? That's really nice of them. Maybe we could help wash the cars, too...or at least some of *you* could. I can't get my stomach wet." *Oops. Did I really let that secret slip?* I wondered how she knew about shortening chronic kidney disease to CKD. I guess she heard it from her sister's friend.

"I'm up for washing cars," Caroline said. "They already started painting signs for it last night." I didn't expect high schoolers to help. *Very cool.*

Eli dragged Jamal and a classroom tablet over to me. "Jamal, let's start rolling on Nick's video." He went into producer mode. He loved Eddie's YouTube idea.

"Okay. You guys work it out," Jamal said, "and I'll be back shortly to film it."

I reminded Eli, "We have to figure out what to say first."

"Yeah, I've been thinking about that. I have some stats for us to use." *Maybe this time Eli's stats will be helpful instead of just plain scary.*

"Good idea. We'll be sure to include some of those. My little sister made up a short poem. We could tweak it and maybe use parts. It's kinda catchy."

"Yes, we need a jazzy jingle to amp our production—you know, like they do in the ads."

I threw one out there. I tried to say it like the rappers do: "I'm the Kidney Man. My blood's positive B. Have a kidney to spare? Please give it to me!"

"That was good, Kidney Man. Say it again, and I'll give you some background music this time." The professor started his famous, or infamous, beatboxing. It did add a nice touch to my little verse, even if the rhythm was off.

"Hey...we might be onto something." I kept it going. "I'm on the donor list, but it's very, very long. I need a new kidney so I'm singin' this song."

Eli continued, "A hundred thousand people need you to give...if you wait too long, some of them won't live." *Ouch.* Not sure I liked that line, but maybe it had to be said.

Back to me..."Roses are red and those violets are blue. Add a heart to your license...it's the right thing to do."

Eli brought it home..."Decide to help. You can find out how. Make your wishes known. Tell your family now."

"Eli, that was epic. We could take this on the road."

Before we forgot our verses, we wrote down all the lyrics to our little rap. After a few tries, we decided it was pretty good. Jamal came back to record it. He asked, "Where's this video going to be posted, Nick?"

"My brother's putting it on the social media page he designed for me."

"Awesome." Jamal and Eli got even more excited after they heard it was going to go live.

The rest of the day flew by. Even though we had to do other school work, the campaign was front and center on our minds. Sneezy suggested writing an email our families could send to everyone they know. Miss T said we could ask our parents about it as part of the homework. She liked involving our families. "That's a great starting point for putting the word out. Get those letters to the editor finished tonight. I want to send them off to the newspaper tomorrow."

"Thanks, Miss Taylor." One thing I know for sure...news does travel fast these days.

CHAPTER NINETEEN

"Today is gone. Today was fun.
Tomorrow is another one."
—DR. SEUSS

The Kidney Man campaign craze didn't just involve the kids at school. My family dove in head first too. When I got home, I updated Mom on all the progress and showed her the video Eli, Jamal, and I put together.

She said, "I love it, Nick!"

"We barely practiced, but I think it turned out pretty great!"

Eddie came rushing in after school. "Are you talking about what I think you're talking about?"

"Yep…and it's awesome. See for yourself…" I played the video for Eddie.

"You did not disappoint, little bro. This is pretty

amazing." For a change, Ed was actually impressed with something I'd done. He said, "Send it my way. It's showtime!"

I snapped up my phone and quickly sent Eddie the link. Within a few seconds, it went live and played on my very own social media page. I worried about getting *likes*, but at least I knew my family would click that button for me.

Dad came home from work and kicked it into gear, ordering a bunch of *Save the Kidney Man* flyers. "We won't run out of these anytime soon," he chuckled. "My office works with a company that can produce what we need in a few hours." He even bought magnets to stick on the sides of our cars with the message, "Nick needs a kidney. Can you help?" along with our email address and the National Kidney Foundation's website.

"The students in your class can post the flyers around their neighborhoods and ask their parents to distribute them at work."

"Good idea, Dad. Let's paper the town!"

"We're taking this show on the road...starting with our community," he said.

The next day, the campaign continued in full swing. Every single kid in the class finished the homework. A miracle. Letters were typed and ready to go. Miss T e-mailed all of them to the newspaper that morning. Each of us had to include at least one fact from the big CKD and organ donation poster she taped to the wall.

A few kids got to sit in the Author's Chair to read theirs aloud. That's a big deal in our class. I was surprised that so many kids sounded worried about me. *Another reminder of just how sick I am.*

Bam read his first...

Dear Editor,

I wonder if your readers know that one organ donor can save up to eight lives. I really didn't know anything about organ donation until my friend, Nick, needed a kidney. He has CKD (chronic kidney disease). CKD affects a person's whole body and can make them very sick. You don't need your organs after you die, so why wouldn't you donate them? Think about it.

Thanks,

Sam

Next in the Author's Chair was D...

Dear Editor,

Approximately twenty people die everyday waiting for a transplant. That's way too many. My best friend, Nick, needs a kidney. If he died and we had an empty seat in our class, I would be really mad at the whole world. If someone you loved died, wouldn't you want part of them to keep on living? Please talk to all your friends and family about this.

Sincerely,

Diego

"We have time for one more reader today. Okay, Caroline…"

Dear Editor,

I read that the kidney was the first human organ to be transplanted successfully back in 1954. Being in the same class with Nick made me realize that we need a lot more transplants to happen. We're all worried about our friend. I decided I'm going to donate my kidneys and the rest of my organs. I really hope other people will do the same.

Thanks for listening,

Caroline

"There are so many excellent letters!" Miss Taylor was really impressed. "If I were the editor, I'd have a hard time choosing. I'd have to pick every one of them. Good job writing on such an important topic. Caroline, you have an announcement about the car wash?"

"Yes, my sister's basketball team will set up in the parking lot of the high school Saturday morning. Tell everyone you know to head over there. They need helpers. You can't just get dropped off though…bring a parent."

"Thank you, Caroline. How many of you plan to volunteer?" Hands went up everywhere, including mine.

"Great," Caroline said. "Me too!" *Glad to hear that.*

The next morning at breakfast, Mom gulped down her coffee and started to read the newspaper. She let out a big squeal. "Nicholas! Look at this! I think the editor published every letter you kids sent. An entire section is devoted to your *Save the Kidney Man* campaign. I'm so proud of you!" She did her *plant the 5 kisses on the face* thing.

I grabbed my tablet and pulled up the article. "I must be dreaming again!"

"I'm going to go buy every newspaper I can find before they sell out." She jumped up and scooped up her car keys. *Whoa...she was serious about that.*

"Thanks, Mom. Good idea." I was as happy as the day I shot the winning basket in a tie game right at the buzzer. I took our copy of the newspaper and hopped on my bike.

This time I waited for Diego instead of the other way around. "D, look at this...our letters made it into the paper!" Diego grinned so hard I thought his face would split right open.

"Are you kidding? Did they print mine?"

"Front and center, buddy." I knew every kid would want to know if they made the cut. I mean, how many ten-year olds can say they had something published in the newspaper? We couldn't wait to show everyone at school.

We locked up our bikes and ran over to the basketball court. Bam was shooting hoops with Jamal. "Guys, take a look at this!" I opened the paper to the headline splashed across the top of the page in big letters: *Students Know Importance of Organ Donation.*

"Wow! You did it, Kidney Man!"

"No, Jamal, WE did it. We even got two pages!" Jamal and Bam ran around in circles. They dashed from group to group on the playground telling anyone who would listen, "We did it! We made it into the newspaper! Every single one of us!"

The bell rang. Our noise level was out of control when we entered the classroom, but Miss Taylor didn't even care. She'd seen the paper that morning too, and she beamed with pride.

My mom stopped by with a copy of the editorials for each of us. We examined every word of every article. The support for our *Save the Kidney Man* campaign was off the charts.

Sam said, "I never thought adults cared that much about kids' opinions. I guess I was wrong."

George added, "I know one thing...the people in this town care more about organ donation today than they did a week ago, and we're responsible for that." This definitely hit home with Sneezy. It stinks that his dad never got the heart transplant he needed.

I said, "It's really something, isn't it, George?" I wondered if our *Kidney Man* campaign could actually make a difference in this world or if I was getting ahead of myself.

We did our usual stuff that day—math problems, science experiments and play practice...but nothing compared to the way the day began.

When I got home from school, we checked on

Grandpa and gave him an update. He sounded so much better. "Put me down for a handful of those flyers. I'll find spots for them when I take my walks around these halls. This is a busy place...you just never know who will see them." I knew he'd plaster those walls with flyers in no time. *I'll feel even better when I see Pops swatting flies again on the back porch.*

CHAPTER TWENTY

"Today you are you,
That is truer than true.
There is no one alive
Who is youer than you..."
—DR. SEUSS

Eddie flew down the stairs and put his face right in front of mine. "Come with me right now!" He wore a big smile; otherwise, I'd have thought he wanted to yell at me about something.

"What's happening?" He dragged me up the stairs and over to his desk. "Come on, Eddie. Give me a little hint here."

"Look at this..!" He pointed to my social media page on his computer screen. The expression on his face made me wonder if we'd just won the lottery or something. I looked at the number of *likes* and *views* of my video, and I thought, "Am I seeing things?"

He screamed, "You're famous!" I was stunned. Eddie and I stared at the screen, mesmerized at the number of *likes* we saw.

"Mom! Come in here...quick!" Mom and Katie ran in to see what was going on.

Eddie's voice reached a fever pitch. "Nick's video was already viewed over 30,000 times. The Kidney Man went viral!"

Mom leaned in to take a closer look at the screen. "Does this mean 30,000 people actually watched your video? How's that possible?"

I said in disbelief, "We just put it up there a couple days ago! I don't even know 300 people, let alone 30,000!"

Eddie was elated. "It's crazy, isn't it?"

"Wait till I tell the kids at school. They'll flip over this news!"

"To tell you the truth," Eddie said, "my friends and teachers will be pretty impressed too. You're a sensation, little brother!" Eddie high-fived me. "And you couldn't have done it without my help."

I said...and I meant it, "You're right about that." We got ready in a hurry. We couldn't wait to tell our friends.

Diego and I headed out on our bikes, and I filled him in on our viral video. "No way!"

"I swear...I'm not exaggerating one little bit." We pulled onto the playground and locked our bikes to the rack.

Sneezy ran over, looking like he'd just run a marathon—he could barely catch his breath. He managed a whisper, "Guys, there's a truck here from Channel 8!"

I whispered back, "Are you serious, Sneeze? Do you think they're here for our campaign?"

He shrugged to indicate that he didn't know.

With that, we all took off to check out the truck. "Yep, it sure is Channel 8. I'll bet Molly's dad's here."

A couple minutes later, we saw Miss Taylor walk onto the playground, looking for someone. We ran toward her, and she motioned at us to hurry. "Nick! There you are. I have a big surprise for you." *I knew it! I'll have to thank Molly for this one.* "Molly's dad is here and wants to interview you for the news."

Between sneezes, George looked star-struck. "You'll be on TV, Kidney Man!"

"Should I wear my Mercutio cape? That'd make me *look* more like Kidney Man."

"Sure, Nick," Miss Taylor said. "It's in the classroom closet. Molly told her dad all about your campaign. He said he also saw a video? Is that the one you guys made in class?"

"Yes, my brother started a social media page for me, and he uploaded our video. People viewed it like crazy!"

"Wow! Congratulations! Well, let's get you inside to talk to Mr. Cooper." Diego and Sneezy tried to follow us. Miss T winked. "Nice try, fellas."

Molly's dad was talking to his camera guy when we approached him. "Here's the man of the hour. I recognize you from your video, Nick. I'm sorry to hear about the challenges you're facing with your kidneys. We're all pulling for you. Looks like the video you posted was a big hit."

"It's up to 30,000 views," I said proudly.

"Actually, it's closer to 40,000 now."

I was stunned. "You're kidding! That's hard to wrap my head around."

Miss Taylor said, "Nick, we just spoke to your parents. Mr. Cooper wants them to participate in the interview. They'll be here shortly."

The crew set up their equipment in the hallway by the principal's office. They told me to take a seat, so I sat and watched them work.

My parents got to school in a flash, even though Dad had to leave work.

As soon as I saw them, I blurted out, "I have to answer questions on camera? How many people actually watch the news anyway? Thousands?"

"You'll do great, son." Dad made a funny face. "We have to answer questions too...let's think about all the good we're about to do and focus on that." Mr. Cooper came over and introduced himself to my parents. He said we'd be on air in a couple minutes. *Aagh! So nerve-wracking.*

A crew member started a mic check, and then Mr. Cooper spoke, "Testing. Testing 1...2...Testing." *Sounds to me like it works.*

Mom and Dad had that nervous laughter going

on—the kind where you grin 'cause you don't know what else to do. Mr. Cooper said, "Rolling in seconds. My advice: tell Nick's story and put the spotlight on his campaign to raise awareness about organ donations." *Molly's dad sure sounds like a pro.*

Mom said, "We can't tell you how much we appreciate you promoting Nick's story."

He looked my way and smiled, "Of course. Any friend of Molly's is a friend of mine." *Oh boy. Don't I feel like a jerk.*

The camera guy gave a 3...2...1 signal with his fingers...then..."Action!"

Molly's dad spoke with a booming TV voice as he fired questions at Mom and Dad. They did a great job answering. They talked about the team of professionals who were helping us. Then Dad said, "Every morning I wake up and wonder if this is the day we'll get the news that there's a kidney for Nick." *That makes two of us.*

Mom chimed in, "Nick hardly ever complains, and his sense of humor helps us cope." *Good to know...although I did my share of crying about it.* I'd be lost without my family. Even fast Eddie.

"Let's bring Nicholas into this conversation." *Uh-oh. Hot seat.* "Nick, I hear you and your classmates began a *Save the Kidney Man* campaign. Your video's gone viral, and all your classmates' editorial letters about organ donation have been published in the newspaper. Where did you come up with these ideas?"

"First of all, my brother and I decided on a nickname

for me: *Kidney Man*." I held up my picture and said, "People at home might want to take a look at this picture I drew of my Kidney Man character..." Mr. Cooper gave me a nod of approval. "You'll notice he's wearing a cape because I wanted to show him being as strong as a superhero." I set my picture down and turned so everyone could see my cape. "I'm wearing a cape today also because, with a ton of help from my family and friends, I'm going to come out of this stronger than ever. My grandmother made it for me to wear when I play Mercutio in *Romeo and Juliet* at the end of the school year. You can come back and see the play if you want." I kinda forgot we were on the air for a minute there. *And, what was his question again?*

He chuckled. "Nick, I'll definitely come back and see your performance. So why a campaign? What do you hope to accomplish?"

"Going through this made me realize there aren't enough organ donors. I want people to know that lots of us are waiting for organs...kidneys...livers...hearts...lungs...even eyes. Maybe someone out there watching will decide to donate a part of them when they die. Some might even want to be living donors." *Oh yeah...I'm on a roll.* "I hope people hear this story and make up their minds to help."

"Your teacher showed me an essay you wrote recently in which you made three wishes. Will you please read those wishes?"

"Sure." I sorta forgot about that paper. She must've

kept it locked in that mysterious drawer by her desk. "Well, I won't read the whole thing 'cause it's kinda long. But, basically, my first wish is for good health and happiness for my family—they really deserve it after all they've done for me. My second wish is for world peace—you know because we all want that. And, last but not least, my third wish is for a new kidney—so I can be like other kids." He moved the microphone away from me and went solo.

"There you have it. Let's help Nick make that third wish a reality. Sign up at your local DMV to express your desire to be an organ donor. Don't forget to call the people you love and let them know you want your organs donated if something happens to you. This is Rich Cooper reporting from Harris Elementary School."

Phew. I can breathe again. I have to admit it was pretty exciting! I'd hoped our message would make a difference. I had a sneaking suspicion it would. I could feel it in my bones...and right down to my nasty old non-working kidneys.

CHAPTER TWENTY-ONE

*"Unless someone like you
cares a whole awful lot,
nothing is going to
get better. It's not..."*
—DR. SEUSS

When Mom and Dad said they were helping Grandma take my grandfather home from the hospital, I begged to go along. "Please! I have to tell him all about the interview. It might cheer him up."

Dad said, "Nick, we'll probably have to hang around there a while before the doctor releases him. I know how much you hate waiting."

Mom added, "You'll ask every five minutes when the doctor's coming. You know how that goes." I promised myself—and my parents—that I wouldn't say a word, even if I was bored out of my mind. For some reason I couldn't explain, I really wanted to get to that hospital.

She finally consented. "Okay, you can come with us, but take that new library book along so you'll have something to read."

As soon as I walked into my grandfather's hospital room, I noticed he looked way better than last time. We even did our special handshake. Finally, things felt almost normal. "Hey, Pops, feeling fit as a fiddle again?"

"You betcha'! And look at you, pal. Can I get your autograph before your spot on the six o'clock news tonight? You're on there for a good reason...not because you're going to jail or anything." Grandpa always joked that people on the news were usually in some kind of trouble. It was nice to hear him kid around again.

"No way. No jail time for me." We both cracked up laughing, mainly because it was great to have him feeling better, even if that meant he was back to razzing me a little.

"He handled the interview like a pro." I could hear the pride in Mom's voice.

Dad said, "Let's turn your TV to channel 8, Joe. We can't miss Nick's television debut. Actually, Maur, it's our TV debut too." He laughed.

"Good idea, Barry." Pops handed Dad the remote. "Get that TV fired up." *Neither of them would miss this for anything.*

Dad chimed in..."Bonnie, even the cape you made is famous now." He likes to make Grandma laugh...and she does laugh every single time, funny or not.

Gram said, "Maybe our cape will be the next big seller in stores." She gave me a little wink.

"Shh...There's Molly's dad talking about Nick. He sounds just like he does in person." Dad was so excited about this.

"And that's coming right up after the break. You don't want to miss it." Suddenly, I felt like maybe I *did* want to miss it. As a matter of fact, I wanted to escape that room.

"I'll call Eddie and have him record it for us now so we'll have a copy." *Good idea, Dad. Maybe I'll watch it later when I'm alone and less embarrassed.*

"Do you have a buck, Mom? I wanna go grab some water out of the machine."

"Nick, right now? You won't see your segment, honey. Why don't you wait until after it's over to get the water?" I looked at her, but I didn't say anything.

"Bonnie, do you have a dollar to give him? He doesn't want to watch it now, and that's okay, isn't it Maur?" I was glad Pops had my back. "When I was your age, we didn't buy bottles of water; we drank from a water fountain." Gram rolled her eyes like she always did when Grandpa talked about the olden days. She dug into her purse and pulled out a handful of change.

"Thanks, Gram. I just feel weird about watching this right now. I'm going to take a little walk and see if I can spot any of our flyers in the hallway."

"You can always watch the program later." Mom might have been just a tiny bit worried about me, but really, I was fine.

Just as I expected, Pops had plastered those flyers all over the place.

I veered off into a little family sitting room where I spotted a machine to buy water. I bought a small one, then looked up. So much for my big plan of not seeing my face on the news, 'cause there I was—as big as life— on a TV in there. I turned away from the screen, but I couldn't help it...I had to turn back around and look. I put my hand over my face and peeked out with one eye.

At first I didn't notice the lady sitting in the corner of the room crying. I wondered what was wrong, but Mom said never to stare. I turned up the volume on the TV. I thought the background noise might make her feel better about bawling. I guess she heard the voices on the newscast, 'cause out of the corner of my eye I saw her glance at the screen, then at me, then back at the TV. She did that a few times before she finally said, "Sweetheart, is that you in the cape?"

"Yes, ma'am. I'm Nick...A.K.A. Kidney Man." I didn't smile or anything 'cause I was too wrapped up in see- ing myself on the screen.

The corners of her mouth turned into a weak smile. "You look pretty good up there."

"Thanks," I said, pretending it was no big deal. I saw Mom and Dad on the screen talking to Mr. Cooper. "Those are my parents. I'm waiting for a kidney to be donated to me." For some reason, I added, "I can't wait forever." She started not only crying a little, but sobbing. *Oh, man.* I wasn't even sure what I'd said to trigger that, but I got her a tissue. "I'm sorry. I didn't mean to upset you."

I sat down in the opposite corner of the room. The story was still rolling with Mr. C giving statistics on organ donation. The lady called over to me and said, "You didn't make me cry, love." Her eyes were red and swollen. I spotted the crumpled tissue in her hands. She used it to dab at her eyes, then she spoke again. "You see, my son was in a bad motorcycle accident this morning, and he's not doing well at all. Now, I have a big decision to make." I walked over to her again, but this time I sat down in the chair right next to hers and didn't say a word. I thought maybe if she wasn't all alone, she might feel better, but she kept on crying.

Mom peeked around the corner. "Nicholas, there you are. Is everything alright?"

"Sorry, Mom. I'll be right there." My mom looked confused but stepped out.

I kind of surprised myself when I leaned in and gave the lady one of those three-pats-on-the-back hugs. She patted me a couple times too. "I'm very sorry about your son. I'll bet he's really cool since he has a motorcycle." She cried some more, then held my hand pretty tight.

Through her tears she said, "He *is* very cool." I gave her another tissue. "He would like you—and if he had a chance to give you a kidney, I know he'd do it." She looked me right in the eyes. "Nick...your name is Nick, right?"

"Yes. You can call me Kidney Man though."

"Nice to meet you, Kidney Man. My name is Barbara Briggs." I reached out to shake her hand. "I think you just helped me make a big decision, and for that, you are forever my angel." I wasn't sure what she meant, but she looked a little happier than she had a minute ago.

I walked over to my mom. She said, "Your grandfather's all set to go home." She put her arm around my shoulder and whispered in my ear, "How did I get so lucky?" I guess she overheard my conversation with the lady. *Now we all know where my snooping comes from.*

The next day, Christina stopped by our house. Mom had just made breakfast for me, so the two of them sat at the kitchen table and drank a cup of coffee while I ate.

"What are you doing here on a Saturday?" I asked. "Don't you ever get a day off?"

"Nick, I wanted to talk to you in person about your Kidney Man campaign. You really are something, you know that?"

I gave her a confused look. "Did you see me on TV last night?"

She cracked a smile that made her eyes light up, and then she flashed her white-as-cottonballs teeth. *I'll bet she brushes twice a day and flosses. I always seem to forget the flossing part.* "I'm sure tons of viewers tuned in, and you were great!" Christina was the kind of person who always left you feeling a little better than she found you. "I came over to tell you something important. Sometimes, when I'm working at the hospital, I help families who are going through a rough time." I *already know she's good at that.* "When you visited the hospital yesterday, do you remember meeting a lady in one of the waiting areas?"

"I sure do. Barbara Briggs. I met her in the family room. She was in there crying. She was sad because her son was hurt pretty bad in an accident."

"I know you spoke to her because she described you, and I told her we were old friends." I was glad Christina thought of me as a friend. "Nick, I'm sorry to have to tell you this, but her son passed away last night." It felt like someone knocked the wind out of me. I closed my eyes tight and wished I could've met him. "But, she told me that, at just the right time, a certain young man walked in during the midst of her grief. You, sir, helped her make the decision to donate her son's organs."

Christina probably knew I had tears in my eyes, but she acted like she didn't notice. She said, "Your interview on Channel 8 happened at the exact same time she had to decide what to do. She feels you were an angel sent to her." *That's why Barbara Briggs was crying. It all makes sense.*

"I told her about my *Save the Kidney Man* Campaign, but I hope I didn't make her feel worse. Maybe I shouldn't have bothered her."

"You didn't bother her at all. In fact, it was just the opposite. She wanted me to thank you. You should be proud of yourself for taking your own challenge and turning it into something positive."

I had a ginormous lump in my throat. I felt sad and happy at the same time. Christina leaned over and put her arm around my shoulder. "It's okay to cry, Nick." A tear dripped down my cheek. *Sheesh.* "You have a big heart, and sometimes that big heart is going to break for people you meet along the way." *That's the truth.*

She got up to leave as my mom came in and said, "We better get a move on, Nick, if we're going to help at the car wash this morning."

Christina laughed and said she'd better be the first one in line. "People will soon write notes in the dirt covering my back windows!"

We heard a knock and saw Diego looking at us through the screen door. "*Hola*, Ciceros..." D was right on time and ready to hit the road, buckets and sponges in hand.

"Let me grab my stuff. We'll load it into our car since my mom is driving. D, you aren't going to believe this story." I was anxious to fill him in on Miss Barbara.

"Walk and talk, *chico*. We need to move it." Diego was all business for a change. When I told him about Mrs. Briggs donating her son's organs, he dropped his sponges and bucket.

"No way!" He couldn't believe it.

"I know. We'll have to tell Bam that adults really *will* listen to a bunch of fifth graders."

CHAPTER TWENTY-TWO

> "It is fun to have fun,
> But you have to know how."
> —DR. SEUSS

We pulled into the parking lot where the car wash was already in full swing. Those high school girls don't waste time.

I was stunned when I saw all the kids holding up signs that said, "Save the Kidney Man!" just like my dream. I had mixed emotions because, on one hand, I absolutely couldn't believe so many people cared enough to be there. But on the other hand...it hit me that I was really sick. Sometimes, I managed to forget that.

"You must be Nick..." Caroline's big sister shook my hand. I knew who she was 'cause I went to a couple of her basketball games. She smiled as she introduced herself to Mom, and in a voice as sweet as her sister's said, "I'm Sarah." I think she was kind of in charge of the car wash because everyone kept asking her questions.

"Remember, Sarah, Nick can't get wet, so he'll have to do something away from the water." *Geez...did you have to say that to a teenager?* Mom would remind me a hundred times that I couldn't get my catheter wet.

Sarah gave us an understanding look and said, "I have the perfect job for him—taking the *dinero*." *She must be in Eddie's Spanish class.* "We don't want the dollar bills to get wet either, so it's an excellent match. You can collect the money and direct cars. Maybe you can help him at that station, Mrs. Cicero?"

"I'd be happy to do that. Thank you." Mom and I set up shop at the entrance of the parking lot. Diego went right over and got in the thick of things. He immediately started firing wet sponges at people. *No wonder he was in such a big hurry to get here.* Sneezy started washing cars, but the soap made his allergies act up, so he moved over to drying detail with Bam.

Caroline came toward us. "Hi, Nick. My sister thought you and your mom could use another person over here."

"That'd be great, Caroline!" *I'm starting to sound like a normal person when I talk to her. This is good.*

The high school girls blasted their music. Mattie Fire and Mattie Ice dressed in their dance gear and put on a little side show for the customers in the waiting area. At one point, even my mom danced to some song she said was one of her favorites, and it was about working at a car wash! The weather was nice, and the vehicles were lined up. It was a success.

When we got back to class Monday morning, Caroline told us the grand total of the proceeds earned from the car wash. I was amazed that we made $343.50, but we didn't do it just for the cash. Sure, we were thrilled to make some money for the Kidney Foundation, but the goal of this fundraiser was to get the word out about CKD and encourage organ donation. Who knows...maybe there was another Miss Barbara there Saturday getting her car washed.

With each passing day, I felt more tired and less interested in school. Miss Taylor walked toward my desk a lot now, especially if I put my head down. "Nick, you okay?" I'd nod and we'd move on.

Maybe it was my imagination, but even Mr. V seemed to be keeping an eye on me out on the playground. "Hey, Mr. Cicero. Why don't you go see Nurse Abby and get yourself a cold drink of water? It's a warm one out here today." *You can say that again.*

Diego and I stopped riding our bikes together. I asked Mom if she would just drop me off at school on her way to Katie's preschool. D kept riding his bike. That was okay by me, even though we both missed hanging out in the mornings.

Spring break was close. We all had that feeling you

get just before a vacation starts. You know, the one that makes you want it to come faster. The hands on the clock moved slower than turtles. I just wanted to hurry home after school and watch game shows with Grandma. D even teased me, "Are you turning into some kind of old guy, Nick?" Maybe I was 'cause the couch called my name every day when I heard the sound of that spinning wheel.

My family and I had a big trip planned for our week off school. We sat around the kitchen table talking about it. Dad said, "I'll be waking everyone up at six bells Saturday for our vacation, so be ready. I'd hate to leave without you." He never tells time like everyone else. He always says *bells* instead of *o'clock*, but I think he's just trying to be funny.

"Don't weave me here!" Katie looked scared.

Eddie spoke up, "Never fear, little sis. I'm pretty sure Dad was kidding about ditching us."

Five-hour drive or not, I couldn't wait to see that ocean again. "Mom, did you rent the same beach cottage we had last time?" I loved the place we'd stayed in before: a two-story right on the beach.

"Sure did, Nick."

"I'll miss going into that ice cream shop though."

"I know, honey. I'm sorry about that." They had flavors I'd never even heard of, so it was always tough to make a decision. I usually ended up with a triple-decker cone that dripped all over the place. With my crazy diet, the ice cream shop was off limits, but a kid can dream.

The cottage sat along the boardwalk where a bunch of people ride skateboards and bikes. Eddie always landed in the middle of that action. Katie had her shovels and buckets already packed. She planned on collecting seashells and making the best sand castle *ev-ah*.

Velcro always goes to the beach with us. He's good in the car as long as he can feel the breeze on his face. Of course, we wouldn't think of leaving home without his favorite frisbee. It's all chewed up, but he's obsessed with it. We take it down to the beach, and whenever we can pry it out of his mouth, we throw it up in the air and watch him jump as high as he can to grab it.

Even though we were going on a trip, I couldn't take a vacation from my dialysis. Good thing my cycler's portable. Mom set it up so everything we needed would be delivered to the beach cottage. It was a little bit of a hassle, but it beat staying home altogether.

I usually spent a lot of time playing in the waves and biking on the boardwalk. Instead, I was looking forward to sitting on the balcony with Pops, playing checkers and building skyscrapers with our bricks. At least I could still watch the waves and listen to them crash against the shore. That puts me in some kind of trance. The Pacific Ocean seems to go on forever. Since I'd be missing out on doing some of my favorite things this time, I'd have to try hard on the vacation to keep my eye on that *elusive* prize Dr. Dave talked about. We learned that word in Language Arts—it means difficult to find. Yep. My new kidney was elusive all right. *Hope that changes soon.*

CHAPTER TWENTY-THREE

"If you get a chance, take it.
If it changes your life, let it.
Nobody said it'd be easy,
They just promised it would be worth it."

—DR. SEUSS

I felt good on Tuesday, so Diego and I decided to walk to school to catch up a little. "Only three more days till spring break, D!"

"I know, but don't forget it's April Fool's Day Friday." Diego cackled like a witch on Halloween. "You better watch your back, sonny!" He cracks himself up. "Nick, do you remember that April Fool's joke Mrs. Andersen played on us in second grade?" Sometimes he gets that snorting laughter going and he can't even talk.

"How could I forget?!" I said. "She handed each of us

a copy of that official-looking letter and said, 'I'm sending this note home to your parents today. I want them to bring you back to school every morning during spring break to practice your math facts.' I guess little kids fall for those things. Not me, of course." I kind of chuckled, knowing he would call me out on that little fib.

"Oh yeah, right!" D wasn't having it. "You were practically in tears when you raised that little hand and whimpered, 'But I'm supposed to go to the beach with my family." He kept talking so he could get to the good part. "With a dead-serious face, Mrs. Andersen had asked, 'Nick, what's more important…learning your math facts or going to the beach?' She sure had us going."

I really was freaked out thinking I'd miss our beach trip. "I managed to squeak out 'math facts,' but I thought she was the meanest teacher that ever walked the Earth…too funny!"

"The best part," D grinned, "was when she yelled 'April Fools!' and we all ripped the letters up instantly and threw them in the air. They were scattered all over that classroom. It looked like a confetti rainstorm."

"We even surprised Mrs. Andersen with that reaction."

"Epic prank." D said. "She was an awesome teacher." We still go into her room every year to visit. She always says, "What?! You guys are getting so tall." Ha! A good liar for sure in my case.

The school days dragged on that week. I was glad we had rehearsal for the play to look forward to at the end of the day. Just when I felt like nodding off or going home to rest on the couch, we'd get up and move around, reciting our lines and building the scenery.

Diego and I liked practicing the parts we did together. "Hey, Kidney Man, let's try your big finale again. That's my favorite." No doubt about it…we all liked a good sword fight scene.

"Try not to bust out laughing or trip me this time when you help me walk off the stage, Benvolio!" We both knew that was gonna be tough for him to pull off.

"Don't worry…I can do this…"

It was the scene where I fought with Juliet's cousin, Tybalt, but Romeo got in the way, so I ended up getting stabbed. We clashed our rubber swords around, then Tybalt got me right in the gut. I'd already given him a heads-up about not touching anywhere near my catheter.

I mustered up my best acting skills. The weak voice was actually pretty easy for me that day. "Help me into some house, Benvolio, or I shall faint." *Strange that I'm the one saying this line.* I had to almost fall down so D could act like he was dragging me off stage. Then I turned back and looked at Romeo and the guy who "stabbed" me. "A plague on both your houses! They have made worms' meat of me!" My voice trailed off as I left the stage. I kind of felt like I was one of those big time actors for a minute there.

Miss Taylor watched us and she clapped pretty loud. "Good job, guys!" When it was over, Diego strutted around like a proud rooster 'cause he made it through the scene without tripping me or laughing.

We still had over a month to go before showtime. I had all my lines down. In fact, I pretty much had everyone else's parts down too. When I hear dialogue repeated a bunch of times, I somehow memorize it without trying. If we had the play tomorrow, I seriously think I'd be ready. A lot of other kids needed more time. I guess that's why we started so early to learn everything. Even though Miss Taylor called it a "pared down version of the original play," that dialogue sure wasn't easy. We all felt pretty grown up using the Old English and pretending we were living in another time and place.

When practice ended on Thursday, Miss Taylor said, "Boys and girls, there will be no rehearsal after school tomorrow since it's the last day before spring break. I hope you have a wonderful, relaxing week off...but don't forget all your lines!" *I think Eli would be more ticked off about that than our teacher.*

At home that night, Mom hooked me up to the cycler, just like always.

I thought about how tomorrow might go. "I wonder what kind of April Fool's prank Eddie plans to pull on me." Velcro was the only one around when I said that right out loud. He tilted his head. Talk about a loyal friend. He still stayed by my side every single time I got my treatment. My brother usually did something to me every year on April first, just to be annoying. Diego would probably say a couple stupid things to try and trick me, but I was ready for him.

I turned on the TV in my room and set the sleep timer to shut off when my favorite show ended. Velcro and I both nodded off before the second commercial.

I don't wake up when I hear noises. I mean, my mother has crinkled a plastic water bottle right next to my ear just to rouse me. Those things are so loud…and so annoying. But nothing stirs me. Mom says I barely move a muscle. That's why it was so strange when my parents walked into my room about 5:30 a.m., and I sat right up. They didn't even have to nudge me or say my name.

"Nick! Great news!" *Why are they glaring at me with those happy faces so early in the morning?* My mom kept talking. "The phone rang a few minutes ago…You won't believe this!" Mom was happier than I've ever seen her. "It was Misha, the transplant coordinator nurse at UCLA Medical Center. Your dad talked to her."

"What?" I was definitely in a fog. "What did she want?…Why'd she call so early?"

Dad chimed in, "It was the call we've all been waiting for. We've got a kidney, Nick!" *No way! The team said it would probably take a long time, if ever.*

Then it hit me. "Wait. Is this some kind of April Fool's Day joke, you guys? Did Eddie put you up to this?" *If it was a joke, it sure was a mean one.*

"No, honey. It's very real. Most kids are going on spring break, but you're going to Los Angeles to get a new kidney!" Mom hugged me and bawled at the same time. I knew right then it wasn't a prank. It felt like my insides would burst.

"Whose kidney am I getting?" My head was spinning. I felt a million emotions all at once.

"All we know is it's from an eighteen-year-old boy." I heard my mom whisper, "God bless that family." Even though I was happy about the kidney, that part sure made me sad.

"Does Dr. Dave know about this?" He'd be squirting his tie and laying those red nose beeps on heavy if he did.

"Yes, the nurse said they notified your entire team here in town."

Dad reached up and unplugged my dialysis machine. "Look at that. It says *End of Treatment* on the digital readout." He squeezed me like he was never going to let go. "This time it really *is* the end of your treatment, son." *My very last dialysis treatment.*

Velcro knew something good was happening. He barked and wagged his tail like crazy. He slapped it against the bed so hard, he sounded like a drummer. Maybe that's what woke up Eddie. He burst into my room.

"How come I wasn't invited to this little family chat? And why are you all up making so much racket at five am?"

"Eddie, Nick is getting a kidney! We just got the news."

"Whoa! The Kidney Man is getting a kidney? That's awesome, little brother!" Fast Eddie high-fived me.

"Guess what, Eddie...after my transplant, I'll be the only kid I know who has three kidneys!"

Eddie said, "Two hanging out in your back that don't work anymore and another one given to you by a lost hero who saved the day for Kidney Man!"

We all smiled and cried at the same time. Dad said, "Some heroes wear fire hats or police uniforms, but ours is a special teenage boy who's in heaven...one of heaven's heroes."

CHAPTER TWENTY-FOUR

"And will you succeed?
Yes! You will indeed!
(98 and 3/4 percent guaranteed!)"
—DR. SEUSS

Lucky for us, Uncle Pat worked for an airline company. He booked us on a nine o'clock flight to California, and I'm talking morning, not evening, so we had to get the lead out, as Dad says.

"We've had our plan of action in place for a while now, so everybody knows what to do." My father definitely slipped into morning traffic director mode. "We leave for the airport in an hour, Nick, so shake a leg." *C'mon, Dad. Shake a leg?*

Mom ran on some kind of nervous energy too where she did five thousand things at once. *How does she do that, anyway?* "Eddie, call Grandma and Pops. They wanted to know the minute we heard from UCLA. They're staying here with you and Katie until we get back home. Dr. Dave said Nick should be in the hospital for about a week, if all goes as planned."

"I already spoke to Gram and Pops, and they're on their way over." Eddie seemed proud of himself that he was on top of it. "Not to sound like it's all about me...but are we still going to the beach house?"

"Now that you mention it," Dad said, "the house is paid for and the hospital's pretty close, so I say yes. It's actually the perfect time to have a house nearby. I don't think Gram or Pops would be up to driving the whole five hours to California though, so do you think you could help, Ed?"

"Absolutely," Eddie answered. "You know I'm the best driver west of the Mississippi." He pointed at the three of us with a big grin on his face and added, "I am an adult, don't forget." He always feels the need to remind us of that. *That's debatable.*

Dad added, "Eddie...you need to help your grandparents. Even though Pops is better now, we don't want him to overdo it. Take out the trash and recyclables, walk the dog and clean up after yourself. Remember that list we went over? It's hanging on the refrigerator. Take it with you to the beach. They'll still need your help after you get there."

Normally, that's right about when Eddie would've made some kind of wisecrack, but instead he just

said, "Don't worry about us. I got this covered, Dad."
*Hello…9-1-1? Come quick. Someone has taken over my
brother's body.*

I texted Diego. I figured he'd check his phone as
soon as he woke up. He gave me strict orders, "When
you get the word that your third kidney is making an
appearance, your best friend better be the first to
know." I knew he'd blab it all over school before the
morning bell even rang.

At least I was familiar with UCLA Medical Center since
we'd gone there a few times for tests and to meet the
transplant team. None of them rode in on skateboards,
but they were all pretty friendly. On our first visit, my
parents had filled out a ton of paperwork so I could
get listed. That meant I would be put on a list with
a whole bunch of other people who were waiting for
kidneys. Mom said, "They must've killed a tree to make
all these forms."

Our trips to L.A. were usually like something out of
a family vacation comedy. Dad drove, and we always got
lost two or three times 'cause he'd take wrong turns
and honk at everybody. I thought it was kind of funny,
but my father never cracked a smile…and his face got
real red. I think those *crazy drivers*, as he calls them,
get on his nerves. *Good thing we're flying this time.*

The flight to the Los Angeles Airport, or LAX as
everyone calls it, took about an hour. My stomach was in

one big knot, and I couldn't turn off the million thoughts going through my mind. I tried to concentrate on the game I was playing on my tablet. That didn't work. In more normal times, I'd look at the clouds out the window of the airplane, but I decided to just pull down the shade. I wasn't allowed to eat or drink anything, but that didn't even matter. I wasn't hungry. Just nervous. Dr. Dave had shown me short movies of kids who'd had transplants— the before, during and after stuff. Since I was on the receiving end, I thought about it in a whole new way.

Mom gave me a cool, damp cloth to moisten my lips. They were as dry as the Sahara Desert...or maybe the Mojave. "Honey, are you feeling okay?" She asked me that every ten minutes.

"I'll be glad when this is all over." *The prize is now within reach.*

"Me too, but this is the big day! I know you don't feel lucky right at this moment on your way to a major surgery, but most people end up waiting a lot longer for an organ match. You'll do great, and it'll be over before you know it. I promise." She patted my hand; her hands were ice cold.

We hopped in a taxi and Mom texted Misha when we were about ten minutes from the hospital. She met us in the lobby as soon as we came through the front doors and said, "Your surgery is scheduled for four o'clock this afternoon, Nick." *Sheesh.* Something about having to wait for the final cross-match, whatever that was, though it did sound kinda familiar.

"This is the biggest hospital I've ever seen," I said. *Maybe it really is the biggest hospital in the whole world. I'll have to look that up.*

Misha smiled, "And we have some of the best medical professionals in the country here. They have performed hundreds of kidney transplants for kids just like you. We have one of the highest success rates in the nation. You're in good hands." *Well, at least I'm not dealing with a bunch of rookies.* "Let's get you settled in."

The whitecoats came right on time to wheel me to the operating room. My parents walked with me, one on each side as Dad grabbed my left hand and Mom squeezed the right. None of us said much because we were pretty scared about the operation...this was serious business.

I pushed that thought out of my mind. I really did keep my eye on the prize. I wanted to play and not get tired. I wanted to eat ice cream. I wanted to go swimming and not worry about getting my catheter wet. I wanted to go to bed without being strapped to a machine. If all went well, I'd get my wish and have a good shot at feeling like my old self again.

"Son, your mother and I will be right by your side when you wake up." Dad leaned in for a big hug, and I started crying.

Mom bent down to kiss my cheek and from the look on her face, she was pretty choked up too. This time, she couldn't keep it together. She unleashed her tears, but she did manage to whisper, "I love you."

Then I was off. *Ready or not, here I come, new kidney.*

It seemed like five minutes, but it was actually five hours later when I opened my eyes. That anesthesia stuff is pretty powerful. Mom and Dad were sitting right next to my bed, dressed in paper gowns that helped keep germs away from me. Their eyes smiled behind those disposable masks. *Good sign.* "Everything went great, Nick! You were a champ, and you're now the proud owner of a new kidney!" Mom smiled through her tears.

My voice sounded really weak, but I had to ask, "Can I have a Pepsi now?" They both laughed out loud, but I was serious.

"I'm afraid soft drinks will be on hold a while longer, sport." *Does Dad know that for sure? I think I'll double-check.* "You're in the intensive care unit, so the doctors and nurses will be here 'round the clock to take care of you."

"Are you guys leaving?"

"No way. One or both of us will be here day and night." That was good news.

"A couple other people are here and anxious to see you." Mom and Dad stepped out of my room. I glanced toward the doorway and saw Pops and Eddie. They looked funny suited up in those white gowns and masks. Especially my brother.

Eddie stood by my bed and put his hand on my arm.

It felt kind of comforting. I said, "I guess you got to go to the beach after all."

"Yep. The cottage is twenty minutes from here. It's not the same without you though." *Wow, I think he was actually serious about that.*

Pops tapped his fist on top of mine. "I've got a checkerboard and no opponent...it'll be ready for you when you get out."

"I'm glad I'm in the bed for a good reason instead of you in the bed for a bad reason, Grandpa." I wasn't kidding about that.

"It's just a matter of time before we're on the back porch again killing flies, partner."

Right then, Mom peeked in and said, "Time's up, fellas." They have stricter rules in this part of the hospital.

Eddie remembered, "Oh yeah. I promised Katie I'd give you this." He handed me one of her famous homemade cards. *Looks like she worked extra hard on this one.* "I was her secretary. She told me what to write." I could see she wrote her own name though.

I read it out loud. "Roses are red. Violets are blue. Come home soon." *Okay, a little weak on the rhyme but very special anyway.*

"Gram said to give you a big kiss for her, but I told her I only do hugs." Eddie laughed. "She stayed at the cottage with Katie."

"Tell her there's a big hug *and* kiss coming her way soon from me." They walked out of the room, and I wished I could go to the beach house with them and sit on the deck playing checkers and listening to the waves. You can't have everything though, and this new kidney sure beats a game of checkers.

Before I had a chance to doze off, the transplant surgeon came into the room. I heard a lot of talk about how smoothly it all went. "Nicholas will be very tired today from the anesthesia. We'll monitor him closely to make sure he doesn't reject the new kidney." *I have news for you, Doc. No way am I giving this baby up.*

He turned to me, "You did a great job, buddy."

"Thanks, but I was knocked out, so I can't take much credit. I'm thinking you're the one who did a great job."

He chuckled. "How do you feel?"

"I'm a little achy, but mostly I'm okay. Do I still have my catheter in there?"

"Did you want to keep that?" The doctor winked.

"No way."

"It's gone...you won't have to worry about that anymore."

"I wanted to ask..." I stammered. "I mean...my dad says it's probably still off limits, but I'm praying I can get some Pepsi..."

"I'll tell you what...a little taste won't hurt anything, so I'll ask the nurse to bring you some."

"Really??? Thank you!" *I like this guy!*

"I'll be back again in a while."

One of the nurse's assistants brought in an ice-cold one right away. Nothing ever tasted so good.

I dozed off a lot, but the nurses woke me up for

one reason or another all night long. They hated to keep bugging me, but ICU nurses have an extra load of machines and things to check. A new kidney and a sip of Pepsi—no complaints from this kid.

Even though I pretty much missed out on vacation, the California beach house was close, so my grandparents and Eddie could visit. They even brought Katie along one time after I was out of ICU. She was excited to see the pictures she sent me taped to the wall behind my bed. It was like her own little art gallery. She ran up to my bed before they left and whispered, "I wuv you."

When their week at the beach came to an end, Gram, Pops, Eddie and Katie drove back home. A day or two later, the doctor came in with some good news for me. "Nick, I think you're going to like this...you get to break out of here tomorrow." I couldn't believe my ears. "You'll have to come back for a checkup in a few weeks and you need to visit your nephrology team on a regular basis, but you're going home." I let out a big Yes!!

The next morning, the sun poured through the window like a golden rainbow. Mom turned to me and said, "Good morning, Nicholas. You look bright-eyed today."

"Hi, Mom. That's 'cause I get to go home, right?"

"They're going to release you this afternoon. Uncle Pat got us flights." She was as anxious as I was to get home. "The students return from spring break today, so Grandma is going to school this morning to tell them your transplant was a success. I'm sure they're anxious to hear how it went."

"That's for sure. After all, they had my back all the way through this. Maybe Grandma can ask Miss Taylor to start a video chat with me from the classroom, so I can tell the kids myself."

"If it's okay with the doctor, I think it's a great idea. But you can only stay on for a few minutes. When you're stronger and back at school, you can answer all their questions."

"I'm sure they'll have lots."

Later that morning, Mom's cell phone rang. It was my classmates, so I was pretty excited. When the kids saw my face on the screen, they cheered and clapped and waved like crazy, chanting "Kid-ney Man! Kid-ney Man!" I've heard about people getting chills down their spine...I guess that's what happened to me. As I listened to their applause, it hit me that I no longer had to be on that nightly dialysis leash. Diego and I could go back to our Friday night sleepover ritual. Shoot, I could even pee without a problem now. And, no more catheter so I could enjoy all my sports again. I still had to take a ton of pills every day, but I was used to that.

I felt like a normal kid again. The best part was no more shots. I could even have a Pepsi once in a while. In fact, I could eat just about anything I wanted, as long as I watched the salt.

I was bursting with happiness when I said, "Hi, guys! ...I'm doing fine. No, I'm not...I'm doing great! The Kidney Man got a kidney! The transplant was a big success!" Again, rousing applause broke out, and it looked like some of the girls were crying. I heard Diego's voice the loudest.

Miss Taylor said, "Nick, we couldn't be happier. We all miss you, and we can't wait till you're back with us."

Molly piped up, "I'm going to tell my dad about your transplant. I know he'll put it on his newscast tonight." *Turns out Molly isn't so bad after all.* "He says you have a lot of fans out there pulling for you."

That made me feel pretty special. "Fans? Wow!"

Miss Taylor wrapped it up. Grandma must've given her the word about keeping the conversation short. "Now take care of yourself. We need Mercutio back in time for the play!" *Miss my stage debut? No way.*

"I'll be back to school as soon as they'll let me." I waved good-bye as they cut off the call. I decided right then that I'd listen to everything the doctors and my parents told me to do, whether I liked it or not.

CHAPTER TWENTY-FIVE

"Because when you stop and look around,
this life is pretty amazing."
—DR. SEUSS

Dorothy was right. There's no place like home...and I was happy to be back there. Mom and I were about to take our first post-transplant trip to Dr. Dave's office. She yelled to me, "Nick, we need to get moving. We don't wanna be late." After a couple minutes, she walked in my room and noticed several drawers hanging open. "What are you looking for? We have to go."

"I have a little surprise cooked up for Dr. Dave. Found it! Now c'mon, Mom, you're gonna make us late."

"You're a real comedian, Nick!"

Before we walked into his office, I reached in my pocket. I figured I'd wear the red nose this time. Glad

I found it 'cause I knew he'd crack up when he saw me.

"That's a good one, Nick...at least you didn't get your hands on my tie." He had one of those smiles people get where their eyes smile right along with them. Then he grabbed me and gave me a big bear hug. That red nose flew right off my face. "I couldn't be happier for you."

"Thanks, Doc."

"I got all the reports from your UCLA health team, and things look great so far. Keep up the good work. These first few months are vital to a quick recovery."

Mom chimed in. "His appetite is much better now, Dr. Dave."

"I hear you're a good cook, Mrs. Cicero. I'm sure that helps." *Is my mom blushing?*

"Will I get back to school in time for the class play?"

"You sure will...as long as you stick to the plan and don't do anything crazy while you're recovering." *Maybe he's thinking back to the wheelchair caper with D and Charlie.*

As we left the doctor's office, some water hit the back of my head. "Gotcha!" Speaking of crazy...he just couldn't help himself.

As days turned into weeks, my body kept getting stronger. I walked Velcro every morning and he loved every minute of it.

Since I'd just had major surgery, I couldn't be

around other kids and their possible germs. We sure didn't want my body to reject the new kidney. That meant I'd be homeschooled for most of the remaining school days. I made it completely clear that I had to go back the last couple of weeks so I could be in the play.

I did school work every day, so it wasn't like I just sat around watching TV. A tutor named Mrs. O'Connor came to our house three times a week and taught me all the main stuff in a few hours. Some days we'd video chat on the computer. She always had something interesting to tell me, and we always started our sessions taking turns telling a good joke. "Okay, Nick...here ya go. What did one toilet say to the other toilet?"

"I don't know. I give up."

"You look a little flushed." Every time she gave me the punch line, she slapped her knee and laughed as hard as she could muster.

Without fail, after school each day, Diego called and said, "OK, lay it on me." D loved Mrs. O'Connor's jokes.

It wasn't all fun and games though...we worked hard, especially on math. She said, "You're going to understand fractions inside and out when we're finished, Nicholas." You know what? She was right.

Grandma and Pops came over all the time, and Pops definitely seemed like his old self again. *Too bad for the flies.* My grandparents and I played every card game and board game we could think of. Katie sure was happy to have me around—she had a built-in coloring partner. *If I don't go back to school soon, I'll be looking forward to tea parties.*

I talked to Sneezy and Eli on the phone a few times. "George, I haven't heard you sneeze since we started talking."

"Yeah, I got some new allergy medicine, and it works like a charm. I don't even carry tissue with me anymore."

Eli said, "You know you really beat the odds not having to wait years for a kidney." He was right.

Diego was allowed to stop by after school once in a while, so we played our video games like old times. The biggest surprise was when Caroline called and said she and Molly were coming over to see me. At least I got a heads-up on that one because, I mean, sometimes I stayed in my pajamas all day. I shuddered at the thought of them seeing me in those robot PJs Gram bought.

I actually looked forward to my big brother coming home from school too. He still teased me all the time, but he didn't seem to mind helping me practice my lines for *Romeo and Juliet*. Once in a while, it was even his idea.

"Eddie, I want to go over the part where Benvolio and I try to boost Romeo's spirits. We talk him into sneaking into a big dance party Juliet's family is hosting where everyone has to wear a mask. They called it a masked ball in those days. That's where he meets Juliet. You can be Romeo."

"I think I'd make a fine Romeo," Eddie joked as he twirled a pretend mustache. Maybe Eddie will be an actor when he grows up because Mom always says he has a flair for the dramatic. She's right about that.

I threw him a piece of wadded-up paper to use as our prop. "Romeo, here...put on this mask so no one will recognize us as Montagues." Eddie gave me a look like, *Yea, right. This isn't a mask.* But he played along and held it up to his face anyway.

Ed continued the scene, "It is not wise for us to go, Mercutio." Somehow, that line didn't seem to fit my brother. He'd be the first one up for an adventure...or should I say a *mis*-adventure. We read through the entire scene, and I remembered almost every single word. *Eli will be happy to hear that.*

"Okay, Kidney Man. Party's over. I have to get to my baseball game."

"Can I go with you and watch?"

"You know the answer to that. I wish you could, but too many germs. Maybe I can let you tag along to my next practice because it only lasts about an hour. Hardly anyone shows up at those. Plus, Luke is picking me up today, and there's no room in the car."

I shrugged. Wishful thinking, I guess.

As my brother left, it hit me: I sure was getting tired of hardly ever having my friends around. I had to stay home another week or so, but I was more than ready to get back into action. I never thought I'd be so excited about school. But I had a terrible thought...What if Miss Taylor gave away my Mercutio part? *Nah...she wouldn't do that.*

As soon as Eddie got back from his game, we sat

down to eat dinner. The phone rang and Dad answered. He came back to the table and said, "You really reached a lot of folks with your Kidney Man campaign, Nick. Mr. Manna from the local paper wants to do a follow-up story on you." Maybe he knew the editor who printed all of our letters.

The next day, the reporter arrived on time. Dad appreciated that. My parents sat on the couch, but Velcro and I were comfortable right on the floor. Mr. Manna asked a bunch of questions and snapped a few pictures.

Dad started, "Nick's made remarkable progress since the transplant."

"I'm happy to hear that. How has life changed for you since your son got his kidney, Mrs. Cicero?"

"We have to closely monitor his health. We check his blood pressure and temperature periodically, and he gets blood tests every week. He's a little trooper about all of it." *Mom, did you have to say 'little'?*

Dad added, "He'll take anti-rejection medicine for the rest of his life, but they say his renal function is completely normal now." *Now there's a word I sure know by now. Renal means kidney.* "The good news...his body accepted the new kidney." I gave two thumbs-up on that one.

The reporter fired questions at me next. "Nick, how did it feel when you got the call on April first saying they had a kidney for you?"

I remembered that moment like it just happened.

"I honestly thought it was an April Fool's joke. When you wait so long for something, it's hard to believe that such an important wish could actually come true."

The next morning, before I poured my bowl of cereal, I snatched up the AM edition of the paper. "Wow! Look at this...the story takes up two and a half pages. Hey, Velcro, you look pretty good in these pictures in your new blue collar." He wagged his tail, but I don't think he was too impressed.

Mom got emotional as she read aloud, "The tears come often for Nick's mother when she thinks of other parents giving part of a lost child to one who is living. 'If you love someone, what better way to pass on that love? It can live in somebody else.' There certainly is love living in one lucky fifth grader, Nick Cicero."

Diego called when he got home from school. "Hey, Nick, Miss Taylor brought your article to class. She read it to us and showed us the pictures."

"She did?"

"Yep. It was awesome. Is it okay if I walk over to your house now? I have something to give you."

"Is it okay? Are you kidding? Definitely."

Seeing my friends was one of the best parts of my day.

D didn't waste any time. In less than five minutes, he rang the doorbell. He had a red and blue striped shopping bag in his hand and a huge smile on his face. "I think you're going to like this gift. It's from all the kids in the class."

I yanked out the white tissue paper that was stuck

inside the bag and pulled out a T-shirt. It wasn't just any old T-shirt. "Wow! You guys all signed this?"

"We sure did. And our signatures won't come out in the wash either. It's some special ink. Check out the picture on the front." I couldn't believe what I saw.

"Miss Taylor asked her artist friend to copy your Kidney Man picture onto the shirt. How do you like it?"

"I love it. It looks just like my drawing." The artist wrote *Nick!* on top of the picture and A.K.A. *Kidney Man* under it. "This is the best gift ever, D. Well…except for my kidney. I know what I'll be wearing on my first day back to school."

"The kids ask the teacher all kinds of questions about you. She said when you come back, you can sit in the Author's Chair and answer them."

"I'll tell them anything they want to know."

CHAPTER TWENTY-SIX

"Look at me! Look at me!
Look at me NOW!"
—DR. SEUSS

Back to school! I was nervous and excited at the same time. I even borrowed some of Eddie's hair gel. He'd probably say I took it without asking. I had to sneak into his room 'cause he'd never let me live it down if he knew I wanted to slick back my hair. His teasing was back in full swing. I put on the Kidney Man shirt the class gave me, then checked myself out in the mirror. *Not bad.*

It was great riding bikes to school again with Diego. We talked and laughed the whole way, just like old times. D told his usual knock-knock jokes, and I played along as always. I even laughed at them. I felt so good that morning...just like a normal kid. *No tubes in this stomach.*

"Nick, I have to get a shot after school today. I know you hate those things. I'm dreading it."

"You know, they're actually not so bad." I couldn't believe those words came out of my mouth. "You'll be fine."

He rolled his eyes. "You sure changed your tune, *amigo*."

As we rounded the bend toward school, Diego got more and more excited. "Nick...*Mira!*" *Yep, he's excited.*

I did look..."Wow." An enormous banner hung across the front doors of the building. It read, "Welcome back, Kidney Man!" A bunch of kids from all different grades stood under it. Mr. Vanasco, Miss T, and some of the other teachers were there too. They clapped and cheered when they saw me.

I shouted, "Thanks, everyone!!" I don't think they realized I was about to burst into tears...the happy kind, I mean. *Phew! Saved by the bell.*

We headed into school, under the banner and through the doors to our classrooms. Lots of kids high-fived me and patted me on the back. Kids I didn't even know.

Right after the Pledge of Allegiance and thirty seconds of silence, Miss Taylor invited me to sit in the Author's Chair. "Does anyone have a question for Nick?" Every single hand went up.

Jamal's question was my favorite..."Did you get to keep your old kidneys? I mean...are they in a jar at your house or something?"

"It kind of went like this, Jamal..." I drew a little

diagram on the whiteboard to explain what happened. "They left the two bad kidneys inside me and just hooked up the new one. So I have three kidneys now."

"Three kidneys? Cool!" Jamal was fascinated. I think they would've asked questions all day, but the teacher stepped in.

"Okay, we need to get started on our math lesson. Besides, we're probably wearing Nick out. After all, this is his first day back." She smiled at me and said, "Each of us has learned so much going through this experience with you, Nicholas."

"Miss Taylor, I have something for you. Can I get it out of my backpack?" I handed her a plaque that read, *You have a wonderful gift to reach out to others, and I feel fortunate to be one of the people you have touched.* "I signed my name on the back." Of course I added A.K.A. *Kidney Man.* "I know I was lucky to get so much support from you all year. My parents think so too."

Miss Taylor got pretty choked up, and then she said, "I'm the fortunate one. I'll treasure this always. Thank you so much, and thank your parents for me too." I thought Molly would call me out for being a suck up, but I glanced her way and saw her smiling, ear to ear. *Yep...I think that girl has changed. Or have I?*

The rest of May went by pretty fast. We took a bunch of those *standardized tests.* I'd rather do fun science projects than take tests, but I guess teachers have no choice. Anyway, I was glad Mrs. O'Connor helped me understand fractions, 'cause there were a bunch of them on the math test.

We only had two days to go until the final dress rehearsal for *Romeo and Juliet*. All we talked about at recess and lunch was the play. There were little groups of kids all over the place practicing their parts. Of course, Eli, the DD, floated around supervising.

Finally, our last rehearsal. When we walked into the multi-purpose room and looked at the decorated stage, Sneezy blurted out, "Wow!" *My thoughts exactly.* It looked like one of those beautiful castles in a fairy tale. That scenery team sure did a good job drawing and painting.

The art teacher finished building the balcony too, and the kids painted a bunch of hanging flowers and vines all over it. Bam wondered if he'd be able to see Juliet over that tall wall. "Miss Taylor, I don't think this balcony will work. Caroline is kinda short."

Miss T chuckled. "Sam, don't worry. Caroline, there's a sturdy wooden box back there for you to step on. In fact, let's practice the balcony scene now. I want the lighting crew in on this too." She was right...it worked. It really did seem like Juliet was looking out over a balcony. The kids in charge of the lights turned them all off except the spotlight.

Caroline wasn't even in her costume, but she was glowing up there when she spoke to Romeo. "Tis almost morning, you must go. Good night, good night! Parting is such sweet sorrow that I shall say goodnight till it be morrow."

Bam didn't even crack a smile this time. He sure was in character. He just gazed up at Juliet. For a minute there, I wished I was Romeo. Sam said, "Sleep dwell upon thine eyes." Then the stage went dark. I got some serious chills from that scene.

After that, we started at the very beginning and practiced the whole program, start to finish.

When it was over, Miss Taylor said, "You guys are ready! Nice work! I couldn't be more proud of you."

We'd been looking forward to the performance for months, and the big night finally came. So did the rain and thunder. The streets flooded and there were wrecks everywhere. It was like the sky opened up and dropped an ocean on us. *Unbelievable.* Normally, I'd love that kind of day. I'd be the first one to run outside...especially since I didn't have to worry about getting wet anymore. A downpour like that is rare in the desert. It usually only happens during the monsoon season. But tonight? That's what you call bad timing.

Dad and I darted into the rain and hopped in the car. I had to get there early, so he dropped me off at school. "Break a leg, Nick!" That means good luck in the theater world. He headed back to the house to pick up Mom, Katie and Eddie. My grandparents planned to meet them at the school. My sister already had her

Romeo and Juliet puppets loaded into her princess backpack. *Hope she doesn't get any big ideas about running up on stage.*

We all gathered in the classroom, and Eli started with the stats. "We only get 4.17 inches of rain annually in Las Vegas. The amount of rain we're getting now is very unusual." *You have a point there, professor.* He kept talking..."The weather lady said little trees are being uprooted, so a lot of people will probably stay home tonight." *Great. The big night finally gets here and no audience?*

Molly added, "My dad is covering the storm this evening for Channel 8. He planned to film parts of our program for their *Kids Rule at School* segment, but he said to tell you guys he's sorry he can't make it." That was disappointing...but if I survived a kidney transplant, I could make it through this stormy play night.

Our teacher tried to act confident. She said people would still show up, but her eyes told a different story. "Don't worry. The weather might calm down. Anyway, we're pretty sure most of your families will be here no matter what, right?"

Pops said he'd come to the play even if he had to drag out his canoe. "Your grandmother and I will paddle down there if need be." I think he was serious. Not sure I can picture Gram rowing a boat down the middle of Boulder Highway though.

We had a half hour to go before the curtain went up, and the big question was, "Where's Bam?!" He was nowhere to be found. Since Sneezy was Bam's understudy, he would have to play the part of Romeo if Sam couldn't make it. George freaked out. He looked at Miss Taylor and said, "I don't feel too good." *I guess the understudy needs an understudy.*

Just as panic started to set in, Sam blew into the classroom. "Sorry I'm late. We had to go around a flooded street. You know what they say on the news...'Turn around. Don't drown.'"

Miss T looked relieved. The color came back to Sneezy's face. *I guess he had a miraculous recovery.* "No problem, Sam. Glad you're okay. Alright, class. Everybody take a few deep breaths, then we'll head to the backstage area. You're going to be awesome!" One thing was clear. We all had at least a mild case of stage fright.

We could hear the principal welcoming the parents and the other audience members. "With this bad weather, we weren't sure what to expect, but Mother Nature didn't stop any of you from getting here tonight. Looks like we have standing room only." *Oh, geez. That means it's packed.* Even though that was good news, my stomach flopped like it did the first time I went off the high dive at the pool.

Mr. V sure likes that microphone. He continued, "When Miss Taylor told me her fifth graders wanted to perform *Romeo and Juliet*, I thought she'd lost her mind!" The audience must've agreed 'cause they all cracked up laughing. "She definitely proved me wrong.

I watched their dress rehearsal, and all I can say is...you are in for a real treat. Parents, prepare yourselves for the pride you will feel as you watch your children perform. Keep in mind, the students are running the lights and giving the stage directions...they're doing it all. Now sit back and enjoy this wonderful production." *Here we go. Showtime!*

The audience clapped as the principal walked away from the podium. It got very quiet, so we knew the curtain had opened. Tamika played the theme song from *Romeo and Juliet* on the piano while Debbie danced a ballet. *We have some talented people in our class.*

The action started as six kids walked through the audience and up the center aisle to the stage. They wore black hoods and capes. The only lights were the battery-operated candles they carried. They chanted together, "Two households, both alike in dignity. In fair Verona where we lay our scene..." I was glad we got to see it all at dress rehearsal, even though it was kind of eerie.

"Diego and Nick...get ready." The Deputy Director was in hyper-mode.

I whispered, "D, are you nervous?"

"I'm actually more excited than nervous now. Remember, Nick...cool, calm, and collected." He was right. We practiced a lot. *We got this.*

I peeked out from stage left and could see some of the people in the audience as I waited in the wings. Jamal's mom stood against the back wall with her camera. *Wait...who's that next to my parents? Whoa!...it's*

Dr. Dave, Christina and Mary I! I couldn't believe it. They never told me they were coming.

Diego and I were part of the group who had the first line in the play. Our weapons were in place, and we were ready for a brawl. We all shouted on cue, "Down with the Capulets!"

The other side answered, "Down with the Montagues!" Our rubber swords clanked against each other as we battled it out.

Everyone talked loud and slow on stage, just like Eli had drilled into our heads at practice. It seemed like most of the kids knew exactly what to say and when to say it. I went up on my lines in one tiny part—that means I forgot something—but I kept thinking about what the teacher said. "If you mess up, pretend you didn't. No one will know except you, so just keep going." It worked.

I got a lot of laughs with my dialogue. Especially during the part where I razzed Juliet's nurse about what she was wearing. "A sail, a sail…" Nurses in those days wore big, flapping collars, so I teased her, saying that it looked just like the sail on a boat. Shakespeare had my back on those lines.

Molly did a great job as Juliet's mother. She was perfect for the part. Funny how she really isn't that annoying anymore.

The audience laughed and cried and clapped and cheered. I couldn't take my eyes off their reaction to all of our hard work.

The play ended and we started our curtain call. We each went to the front of the stage and took a bow. Believe it or not, we'd even practiced that. Diego and I went out together. We got a lot of applause and some laughs. Eddie whistled for us and Katie pretended her puppets were clapping. Of course, the audience cheered the loudest and longest for Romeo and Juliet. Caroline and Sam were great. Everybody was.

The entire cast and crew took the final bow together. Debbie and Tamika went out front and handed Miss Taylor a bouquet of flowers. She looked kind of surprised. After that, Eli was supposed to close the curtain…but he didn't. It wasn't like him to mess up, that's for sure. I looked over at him, but he didn't seem concerned. I was just about to say something when, out of the corner of my eye, I saw Sam and Caroline walking toward me. *What are they doing?* They grabbed both my hands and dragged me back to center stage. "Guys…we didn't rehearse this!" Sam and Caroline giggled.

D picked up the microphone. As I stood there looking straight out at all the familiar faces, I whispered, "Diego…what's going on?"

He just grinned and whispered back, "You'll see." Then he turned to the audience. "No one could have played Mercutio like Nick. We're so happy he got his kidney transplant and is here with us today. He had us worried for a while there." The audience clapped. I awkwardly smiled and wondered why D was bringing that up now.

Sam came toward me, holding up what looked like a red, silky cape. On the back it had a big, yellow K written in the middle of a blue circle. I couldn't believe it. "Wow!"

"May I?" Caroline reached up and took my Mercutio cape off while Bam handed her the new cape to snap around my neck. I turned so everyone could see. I looked over my shoulder at the audience. Caroline grabbed the mic and said, "Ladies and Gentleman, let's hear it for the Kidney Man!!" She actually hugged me...in front of the whole world. *Sheesh. I know my face is flaming red.* I turned around and saw Sneezy, Jamal and the whole gang—even Molly—cheering and clapping.

Doctor Dave walked toward the stage carrying something heavy. Some kid popped out into the aisle to help him. "Charlie? Where did you come from?" *It was good to see him.*

He gave me a thumbs-up. "Hey, Nick...you scored big with this. Your favorite!" I looked down and saw a case of Pepsi.

Dr. Dave winked and pretended to squirt me with his tie. "Don't drink this all at once."

The kids shouted, "Kid-ney Man! Kid-ney Man!"

D handed me the microphone. "Your turn, buddy."

I looked down at my family and thought of everything we'd been through. Pops' expression gave me a boost of confidence. He put one fist on top of the other and pointed at me. I surprised myself as the words spilled from my mouth. "When I found out my kidneys didn't work, it was the worst day of my life. But, because of so many of you in this room, this is now the *best* day. *Ever.* I hope other people waiting for organs can one day feel this happy. We all worked hard to raise awareness about the need for organ donors. I plan to keep that going. From the bottom of my kidney...thank you." The audience laughed, then gave me a standing ovation. Not bad for my first ever performance. *Yep, those two little words—Kidney Man—definitely changed my life forever. There's no stopping me now.*

WORDS I LEARNED FROM DIEGO AND HIS ABUELA

abuela [uh-**bwei**-luh]: grandma

abuelo [uh-**bwei**-low]: grandpa

adiós [aa-dee-**ows**]: goodbye

amigo [uh-**mee**-gow]: friend, dude

chico [**chee**-koh]: boy

dinero [dih-**nair**-oh]: money

dios mio [**dee**-ows-**mee**-oh]: OMG

estoy bien [es-**toy-bee**-en]: I'm fine

fantástico [fan-**tas**-ti-co]: fantastic

gracias [**grah**-see-ahs]: thank you; muchas gracias [**moo**-chas **grah**-see-ahs]: thanks a lot

hola [**oh**-lah]: hello

mi casa [mee-**kah**-sah]: my house

mira [**mee**-rah]: Look!

nada [**nah**-duh]: nothing

primos [**pree**-mohs]: cousins

que pasa [keh-**pah**-sah]: What's up?

vámonos [**vah**-mo-nos]: Let's go!

Interesting fact: D says that in Spanish, you use one exclamation point at the beginning and one at the end of the sentence. The one before is upside down. Same with the question marks. Pretty cool.

WORDS I LEARNED FROM DOCTOR DAVE AND THE NURSES

anesthesia [an-es-**thee**-zha]: medicine doctor gives a patient to help him or her fall asleep and stay asleep during surgery

catheter [**kath**-i-ter]: a thin tube put into the body to help with medical procedures

cycler [**sahy**-kler]: fills and drains cleaning solution during dialysis

dialysis [dahy-**al**-*uh*-sis]: treatment that can be used to filter the blood when kidneys fail or need to heal

ICU Intensive Care Unit [in-**ten**-siv kər **yoo**-net]: (in a hospital) continuous treatment for patients who are seriously ill, very badly injured, or who have just had an operation

kidney [**kid**-nee]: takes waste out of the blood and makes pee

nephrologist [nuh-**frol**-uh-jist]: kidney doctor

pediatric [pe-de-**at**-rik]: having to do with the branch of medicine dealing with children and their diseases

peritoneum [per-i-tn-**ee**-um]: thin tissue that lines the inside of the tummy/abdomen

phlebotomist [fluh-**bot**-uh-mist]: person who does blood tests

radiology [rey-dee-**ol**-uh-jee]: the science dealing with X-rays or nuclear radiation, especially for medicine

renal [**reen**-l]: relating to the kidneys

X-ray [**eks**-rey]: Powerful forms of energy; can go through substances light cannot; photographs inside of an object, such as a suitcase or human body

AUTHOR'S NOTE

I had the pleasure of teaching Nicholas Cirkosz—the original "Kidney Man"—when he was in fifth grade. Judy and I always wanted to write his story, since he left such a mark on my life. Nick's parents, Cookie and Wally Cirkosz, were very supportive.

While this is mostly a work of fiction, it was inspired by Nick, who lit up the classroom with his sense of humor and infectious personality, all while battling kidney disease. He did get a successful transplant in fifth grade, just as our character did. He created a superhero kidney figure and always signed his papers, "A.K.A. Kidney Man." Nick had a memorable performance as Mercutio in our fifth-grade production of

Romeo and Juliet, and yes, there was a storm that evening. We named the dog in our book Velcro because that was his Dalmatian's name. In a show of support, his classmates rallied around him and wrote "Letters to the Editor" on his behalf. He enjoyed the T-shirt the class gave him with *Nick...#1 Kidney Man!* painted on the front. Nick gave me the plaque described in the book, and I treasure it to this day.

He didn't have a little sister, but he had two older brothers, Mark and Mike, who, according to his mom, enjoyed teasing him. His kidney transplant took place on October 31, not on April Fool's Day. His mom broke the news to him early that morning with these words, "Some kids get candy for Halloween, Nick, but you're getting a kidney."

We were honored to write this book. Nick touched so many lives, and his story remains in our hearts forever. Our hope is that more people who await transplants will get their gift of a life-saving organ donation too.

Karen LoBello

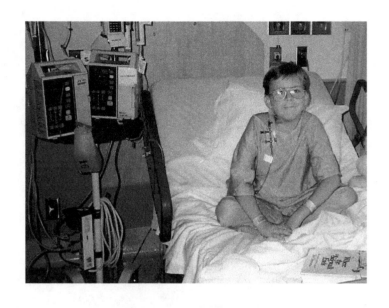

ABOUT THE AUTHORS

Karen is a former teacher who currently resides in Nevada with her husband, Rich, our "unofficial" editor and first reader. She loves to visit her favorite place—anywhere there's a beach—whenever she can.

Judy is a fourth grade teacher who also resides in Nevada, with her husband, Barry, and their two sons, Nicholas and Matthew. She has two dogs, Copper and Verro, who would be very upset if they weren't mentioned as part of the family.

Judy and Karen are also authors of a children's picture book, *The Great PJ Elf Chase: A Christmas Eve Tradition*.

People often ask us, "Was it hard writing a book together?" Our reply…"Maybe it was easier because we're sisters, but we couldn't imagine it any other way."

Contact us at *lovobooks.com*.